WILD
HOUSES

ALSO BY COLIN BARRETT

Young Skins
Homesickness

WILD
HOUSES

COLIN BARRETT

Grove Press
New York

First published in Great Britain in 2024 by Jonathan Cape, an imprint of Penguin Random House UK.

Published simultaneously in Canada
Printed in the United States of America

First Grove Atlantic hardcover edition: March 2024

Typeset in 11/16pt Janson Text by Jouve (UK), Milton Keynes

Library of Congress Cataloging-in-Publication data is available for this title.

ISBN 978-0-8021-6094-2
eISBN 978-0-8021-6095-9

Grove Press
an imprint of Grove Atlantic
154 West 14th Street
New York, NY 10011

Distributed by Publishers Group West

groveatlantic.com

24 25 26 27 28   10 9 8 7 6 5 4 3 2 1

For my mother and father

WILD
HOUSES

PART ONE

1

Dᴇᴠ Hᴇɴᴅʀɪᴄᴋ was lying in the dark on the sofa, laptop propped on his belly, asleep or almost asleep, earbuds bleeding white noise into his ears when his phone buzzed three times on the coffee table and stopped.

He felt the vibrations more than he heard them. He sat up, snapped shut his laptop and put it on the coffee table. The white noise in his earbuds died. He reached for his phone and knew the number before he even checked the screen. Three buzzes meant: *we are here.* He pulled the buds from his ears, cocked his head to listen into the empty night and then he heard it, the familiar noise of the car crawling up the drive, the low burr of the engine, the bubble-wrap crackle of wheels turning slow on gravel.

There was a near-empty bottle of Corona on the table. He drank off the dregs. The Corona was flat and citrus-sour, a wilted wedge of lime curled like a drowned bug in the bottom of the bottle.

The dog, Georgie, snoozing away on the battered red wingback chair, stirred and came awake with a startled yelp.

'Shush now,' Dev said.

Georgie was a tiny, highly strung dog with a candyfloss coat covering a ribcage as fragilely fine-boned as a chicken's. He had demonic yellow teeth, a wizened, rat-like face and a moist, bloodshot, perpetually beseeching stare that half the time made Dev want to punt the thing over the garden wall. Not that Georgie ventured outdoors much any more; ageing, ill-tempered and increasingly unintrepid, the dog preferred the cosily cluttered terrain of the sitting room, where he spent his days mooching from cushioned niche to niche and staring at the TV like an old woman.

Georgie yelped again.

'Stop now, will you?' Dev said, raising his voice enough to draw a chastened gurgle from Georgie.

Dev and Georgie had never much got on, but ever since the mother died and the dog had come to the realisation that Dev was now the sole source of sustenance and what would thereafter pass for companionship available in the house, Georgie had developed, if not an affection, at least a grudging receptivity to Dev's commands, so long as those commands were delivered with sufficient emphasis and contempt. Georgie respected only emphasis and contempt, at least from Dev.

Dev slipped on his Crocs and lumbered into the hallway. An icy diagonal of light had pierced the front door's glass panel, illuminating the hall's green-and-gold wallpaper and the musty foliage of the mother's old overcoats piled up on the coat rack.

Dev drew back the latch and opened the door. The

sensor light had come on, flooding the drive with brightness. Rain flurried like sparks in the light. Drops touched
Dev's face and stuck. The car's engine cut off and the headlights went dark. Dev watched his cousin Gabe Ferdia step
out of the driver door and a moment later Gabe's younger
brother Sketch stepped out of the back and helped, or
rather dragged, a third person out onto the drive. The third
person was a kid, a pale-faced young fella.

'Some night for it,' Gabe declared.

'Are you fucking kidding me?' Dev said.

'I'm afraid not,' Gabe said, squinting beleagueredly
against the flurrying rain and smiling slyly out of his long,
thin face. 'You going to let us in or what?'

The three stood there in the rain, waiting on Dev.

'Come in,' Dev said.

Sketch shoved the kid in the back to get him moving.
He was wearing only one sneaker and carrying the second
in his hand, obliging him to hop a little on his socked foot
across the drive's stony gravel. When the kid was close
enough, Dev could see that his face was marked, a dark
nick, too fresh to have scabbed, lining the rim of one eye.
The boy gazed expressionlessly up at the house, then Dev.

'Nah,' he said.

'Yeah,' Gabe said.

'No fucking way,' the kid said.

He stood in place until Sketch shoved him again. The
kid stumbled in over the threshold. Sketch and Gabe came
in after him. Dev latched the door as the brothers marched
the kid down the hall.

*   *   *

When Dev joined them in the kitchen they had put the kid in a chair by the table. The runner was up on the table, next to the butter dish. Sketch was standing behind the kid with his hands on his shoulders. Gabe had removed and was holding up his jacket, a black bomber with the legend TEQUILA PATROL embossed in gold lettering on the back. With a practised flourish he snapped the jacket, once, in the air, sending the loosest droplets of rain flying from the fabric, then draped it neatly across a chair back. He popped the fridge and began fishing out bottles of Corona, placing four of them in a row on the counter.

The kid looked fifteen, sixteen. His face was pale, blue-tinged as raw milk in a bucket. He was clean-shaven and if it wasn't for the missing runner and the nasty notch over the corner of his eye, he would have looked like any young fella you'd see shaping around the town on a Friday night, punctiliously spruced for the disco; short black hair brushed emphatically forward, and so sodden with rain and product it gleamed like melted tar, the top button of his baby-blue shirt closed clerically at the throat, dark jeans and the scouring bang of aftershave crawling off him like a fog.

'Your foot must be wringing,' Dev said.

'What?' the kid said.

'I said your foot must be wringing.'

The kid looked at his foot. He looked at Dev.

'Such a size of a cunt,' he said.

A hot current ran through Dev. He heard the Ferdias chuckle.

'Dev's a godly-sized unit all right,' Gabe said as he

worked the tops off the Coronas. The depressurising hiss and pop of each bottle cap – pop, pop, pop, pop – overlapped with the tinny clinking of the caps as they bounced on the counter and two rolled off the counter's edge and clinked a second time on the floor.

'The *lambs* on him,' Sketch said, 'like excavator buckets.'

Dev looked down at his dangling hands. It was true. They were massive, as was Dev. When he was on his own, which he mostly was now, he forgot about his size. When other people appeared, they were quick to remind him. A lad who grew beyond a certain limit, beyond certain proportions: people just never got used to it.

'You know this fella?' Gabe asked the kid.

The kid shrugged.

'Never seen him about in Ballina?'

'I'd nearly recall a cunt that huge if I had. Is he seven foot tall?'

'Oh, he's not far off it,' Gabe said, 'but Dev is deceptive. Big as he is, he leaves an awful dainty mark on the world. You'd barely know he was there half the time.'

The kid looked at Dev and seemed to be weighing in his mind the possible veracity of Gabe's remark.

'I want my phone,' he said.

'Never mind about your phone, kid,' Gabe said.

'Here, you, big man,' the kid said to Dev, 'have you the lend of a phone?'

'Phone's out of the equation,' Sketch said, jabbing the kid on the shoulder.

'Dev, let me introduce you to Doll English,' Gabe said. 'Doll, this is Dev.'

'I shouldn't be here,' Doll said.

'That's not a problem,' Gabe said patiently. 'Dev doesn't mind, do you, Dev?'

Dev shook his head.

'We were thinking you might crash here tonight,' Gabe continued.

'No fucking way,' the kid said.

'A bit of manners, now,' Gabe said and looked at Dev. 'That'd be all right, wouldn't it?'

'If you're vouching for him,' Dev said.

'One hundred per cent we're vouching for him,' Gabe said. He grabbed a Corona from the counter. 'You can have this,' he said, extending the bottle to the kid, '*if* you're going to sit here and drink it and be civil.'

'Dev here knows Cillian,' Sketch said. 'Everyone here knows your brother.'

Mention of his brother seemed to placate the kid. He accepted the bottle. Gabe passed a bottle to Sketch, offered the remaining one to Dev.

'I'm OK,' Dev said.

'Go on,' Gabe said, pressing the bottle into Dev's hand.

Gabe took a drink. Doll English took a drink. Sketch took a drink.

Dev took a drink, worked the sizzle of bubbles around his mouth and swallowed.

Sketch Ferdia was twenty-five or so, a couple of years older than Dev. He was a handsome unit with the slick, thirty-euro hairdo of a Premier League footballer and the curated muscle of a gym freak, his big, tattooed arms so lavishly lettered and illustrated they looked like the pages of a medieval manuscript. He had a conceited right-angled jaw, moody blue eyes and a propensity for clouting shams in the head the second he decided it was warranted.

Gabe, by contrast, was skin and bone. He was touching forty but looked ten years older again, with a face on him like a vandalised church, long and angular and pitted, eyes glinting deep in their sockets like smashed-out windows. His was the face of a man who had come through some terrible and consuming privation, and Gabe had, sort of. For the best part of a decade he had shot heroin, with the needle and the strap and the whole shebang, a dedicated feat to pull off this far out in the sticks, because heroin was not an available or popular drug in the West. Dev did not touch anything stronger than beer but he knew that the pharmaceutical tastes of the average Mayoite tended away from those substances that encouraged narcosis, introversion and melancholy – traits the natives already possessed in massive hereditary infusions – in favour of uppers; addys and coke and speed; drugs designed to rev your pulse and blast you *out* of your head.

Gabe had been an exception in this regard. He did finally quit the heroin a couple of years back, but only after he managed to overdose at three separate house parties in the span of a single summer, each time winding up in Castlebar emergency. On two of those occasions, he claimed his heart had stopped altogether – he had been clinically dead – and had to be jolted back to life with those electric paddles to the chest you see in the movies. And though he had since reacquainted himself with certain habits – Gabe took a drink, took a smoke, and would take a hit of a joint if a joint was going – he still considered himself clean because he was off the heroin, and if that distinction was sufficient to meet the man's definition of clean, well, fair enough so, was Dev's opinion.

'Dev here's a Muredach's boy, too,' Sketch said.

Muredach's was the boys' secondary school in Ballina town. Cillian English and Sketch had been a couple of years ahead of Dev. Sketch had never said two words to Dev back then, was nowhere to be seen when things had begun to go bad for him.

'Cillian was a hellion but he had a brain in his head,' Sketch said. 'Honours classes until he was expelled, fair play to him. I'd say you were as bad as me, Dev. Pass everything.'

Dev bristled at Sketch's remark but said nothing. Everyone's assumption was that Dev was thick, for three reasons. One, because he was big, and people thought if you were big, you must be some kind of oaf. Two, because he tended not to say much, and people thought that if you didn't say much you mustn't have much to say. And three, because, yes, Dev had been in all pass classes and had not even finished school, but none of that had anything to do with how smart he was.

Dev was watching the kid. Doll's face wasn't giving much away, his expression stony and remote, staring impassively at the bottle of Corona he was holding between his legs. He cleared his throat.

'Whatever's between you boys and Cillian has nothing

to do with me,' he said in a low voice, not looking up as he said it.

Dev heard a pattering in the hall and Georgie came racing around the corner and into the kitchen. The little dog stopped dead in his tracks, sized up the three new presences in the house and commenced barking, in apoplectic recognition, at Gabe's shins.

'Hello yourself, you bollocks,' Gabe chided.

'Settle down now, Georgie,' Dev said.

Georgie ceased barking and looked around again, nose in the air. After another moment's deliberation the dog approached Doll's foot, sniffed and began zestfully licking at the toe of his wet sock.

Doll sat up in his seat. Slowly, as if the action had nothing to do with him, he lifted his foot and for a second Dev thought he might do something awful, like stomp straight down on Georgie, but he only began to nudge, gently and insistently, at the dog's flank with his toe. And Georgie, instead of taking fright or protesting, rolled over onto his back, exposing the pale pink flesh of his underbelly, the livid seam and knotted grey stub where his poor old ballbag used to be. Doll settled the sole of his foot on Georgie's belly and began briskly rocking him back and forth, coaxing a bout of hoarse, satiated panting from the little beast.

'That dog likes you,' Gabe said to Doll. 'And that dog don't like nobody.'

'That dog don't like me,' Dev said.

'Just let me call the mother,' Doll said. 'She'll be worrying.'

'It's two in the morning, buck,' Sketch said, 'your mother's sound asleep in her *leaba*.'

'She's not a good sleeper. The head does be at her.'

'All the more reason not to bother her at this hour,' Sketch said.

Doll stooped forward in his chair to get a better look at Georgie.

'What breed of dog is this?'

'It's the mother's dog,' Dev said.

'The mother,' Doll said. He showed Georgie his palms, and Georgie, to Dev's astonishment, jumped up and scrambled into the kid's lap, the way Dev had only ever seen him do with the mother. 'I'll ask her so.'

'You can't do that.'

'Cos she's dead,' Doll said.

Dev felt his face flush.

Doll began brushing flat the soft quivering triangles of Georgie's ears. Georgie tried to lick the kid's face. With each curling dart of the dog's tongue Doll jinked his chin fractionally out of reach. 'Serious? You don't know what kind of dog this is?'

Dev said nothing.

'This fella would be some mix of Pom and Jack Russell, I'd say. I'd an aunt had one almost like it. They've delicate enough constitutions for all the noise out of them. They do get tricky lungs when they're older.'

Doll gripped Georgie by his scrawny forelegs and lifted him into the air with the dextrous matter-of-factness of a veterinarian. He pressed his ear to the dog's elongated belly.

'Hear that?' he said. 'What age is he?'

'Will you put my dog down?' Dev said.

'You said he was your mother's dog.'

'He's my dog, now. Put him down.'

Doll guided Georgie back into his lap and released him. Georgie slithered down the kid's knees, retreated beneath an empty chair and from there fixed Doll English with a long, consequential look.

'Animals like me,' Doll said.

'How's Cillian's hand?' Gabe said.

Doll did not look at Gabe but his eyes narrowed as he continued to watch Georgie. He scratched the side of his jaw.

'His hand's fine,' he said.

'He tell you how he got that broke hand?'

'Said he fell.'

'Fell,' Sketch said and grinned.

'That wasn't a pleasant episode,' Gabe said. 'But here, did you ever meet Mulrooney?'

'I don't know,' Doll said.

'You don't know?'

'No,' Doll said, 'never met a Mulrooney.'

'Because that's who Cillian's on the hook to.'

'Who Cillian's on the hook to is none of my business.'

'It is, though,' Gabe said. He took a Ziploc bag from his pocket and tossed it on the table. The Ziploc was bulging with knotty green clumps of weed. 'I'd say you were a popular man at that party.'

'That's nothing.' Doll shrugged. 'That's just bits and pieces for me and my mates.'

'Cillian sort you with that?'

'Cillian doesn't sort me with much these days.'

'No, not so much these days, I'd say,' Gabe said. 'I'm asking do you know Mulrooney because that's who Cillian used to work for. We still do.'

'He never told you how it went south between him and Mulrooney?' Sketch said.

Doll shrugged again.

'I'm afraid your brother fucked up there well and good,' Gabe said.

Dev knew the man the Ferdias worked for, because he worked for him too; what Dev did was sit on drugs for Mulrooney. For almost a year now Gabe and Sketch had been showing up – sometimes every few weeks, sometimes not for months – with a bootful of stuff packed away into sports bags. Dev stowed each delivery somewhere dark and dry and forgot all about it until the Ferdias returned. He had several good storage places; a couple of derelict cattle sheds in the fields down the back lane, or just here in the house if the sit was quick. He was a good sitter because he lived in the middle of nowhere, he never left the house and he lived alone, apart from Georgie. The only people he even saw regularly any more were Gabe and Sketch.

'You hungry?' Gabe said to Doll.

'What?'

'We'll be putting you down for the night shortly. You want some grub first?'

'You've a few on you,' Sketch said. 'Grub'd help.'

'I don't have a few on me,' Doll said. 'I'm fine.'

'You were fairly staggering about when we found you wandering on that street, buck,' Sketch said.

'I wasn't staggering. I was fine. I was heading home. I want to go home.'

'You want something to eat or not?' Gabe said. 'Last chance till morning.'

'Here, I've a microwave thing in the fridge,' Dev said.

He strode over to the fridge and pulled on the door so hard he set the condiments and jars on the shelves rattling dementedly against each other. A jolt of cold white hysteria travelled through him as he realised they had really done it. They had lifted this kid, Doll English, right off the street in the middle of the night and they had brought him here, to Dev's house.

'Dev, how we doing?' Gabe said into his back.

Dev was staring blankly at the blazing sensor light at the back of the fridge. He grabbed a rib sandwich off the middle shelf, tore it out of its packaging, plated it and put it in the microwave.

'Your little beoir went to the party with you. What's her name?' Sketch said to Doll.

Doll drank off the last of his Corona and placed the bottle on the table next to his runner.

'They call them bangs in America,' Sketch said.

'Call what bangs?' Gabe said.

Sketch placed a finger right across his brow. 'The fringe his little beoir has. Yanks call them bangs. She's a tidy bit of kit, all the same.'

The microwave pinged. Dev ferried the hot plate over to the kid.

'Here,' he said.

'You're right,' Doll said to Dev, 'my foot is wringing.'

Doll stood up from the chair and then sat straight back down. He picked the runner up off the table, shot up again and with a sudden fluent motion struck Dev on the side of the head. The blow was not painful but it caught Dev by surprise; too late he ducked and the kid was on him, clawing at his arms and neck and head like he was trying to climb up and over him. Dev let the plate go and tried to get a hold of him but Doll was gone, slid out from under his grasp.

'HEY,' Dev heard Sketch roar.

Doll grabbed the chair Gabe's jacket was drying on and crashed it to the ground. He flung the runner at Sketch's head and dashed into the hall. Sketch ducked and bolted after him, Gabe scuttling close behind.

Dev followed them into the hall. Sketch had already tackled and pinned Doll to the floor. He had an elbow jammed under Doll's chin and seemed to be squeezing his entire weight down on him. Doll's face was turning red, his breath a garbled hiss straining through his bared teeth.

Gabe was just standing there watching, beer still in hand. Georgie was down by Dev's leg, his barking an incessant thin yipping. Dev wanted to say something. To shout out, to get it to stop. He felt his heart lurch and silver motes began to sparkle and crawl in the corners of his vision.

Sketch got to his feet and hoisted Doll up after him.

Doll tried to dart away again and Sketch slipped him into a headlock. The two staggered in a circle around the hall, knocking the coat stand over, bumping from wall to wall.

'Will you stop now, you ASS?' Sketch roared, clobbering Doll in the midriff until his knees buckled. Sketch marched him back into the kitchen and dropped him back in his chair.

'Tell this young fella settle down before I bust him open,' Sketch said as he smoothed his scuffed and pronged hair back into place.

'Now what on earth was that supposed to achieve?' Gabe said, righting the upended chair and squaring his jacket back into place on it.

'I want to go home!' Doll said.

'Didn't I ask you to sit here and have a drink with us and be civil? Wasn't that all I asked?' Gabe said.

Doll was hugging his stomach, shoulders drawn tight. Sketch's punches would have winded him something awful. His shirt was ripped at the shoulder, top buttons popped and collar askew. He looked once around the room, at Gabe and Sketch and the dog, and Dev, and drew his hands up his temples and pulled his head down onto his knees. He pressed the ends of his fingers against the back of his skull, so hard his knuckles began to whiten. His breathing was quiet but became ragged, and for half a minute that was the only sound in the room, Doll English's breaths going in and out in a low, ragged rhythm, his face buried in his lap and his shoulders rising and falling in jerks.

Dev was concentrating on his breathing and trying not

to blink too much. He had almost lost it in the hall, but his heartbeat was back under control. In the corners of his eyes the silver motes were going away, dwindling to black filaments and winking into nothing.

'I was thinking we'd stick this fella in the basement,' Gabe said after a while.

The basement. They had really meant it then, about keeping the kid here. There was another moment of quiet and Dev realised Gabe was looking at him, expecting some kind of response.

'The bed needs making,' was all he could think to say.

'So go make it,' Gabe said.

The spare bedding was in the press on the upstairs landing. The press was small and dark and still smelled faintly of the mother. He pulled out a sheet from a stack of sheets, a heavier bedspread of scratchy wool, a sleeveless pillow grainy with must. The pillow was torso-sized, its stuffing wadded into lumps, like muscle that had lost its definition.

The kitchen was still quiet when he came back into it, Gabe tipping away at his Corona, Sketch's eyes boring into the back of Doll's head. Doll's head was up out of his lap and his hands were hanging between his legs, his cheeks flushed, the skin under his eyes pink and welted. Dev placed the bedding on the table and softly punched the goitred shape back into an approximation of a pillow.

The basement door was set into a recess in the wall next to the fridge. Dev pulled the door open and reached into the chilled dark for the light switch. The basement bulb was naked, stubbled with dust motes that singed as it warmed up, leaving a faint, silvery smell of incineration in the damp air. A dozen steps led down into the low, cramped room. From the top of the stairs Dev could see the entire space. The floor was raw unpainted concrete that looked as cold as a lake, the ceiling barely six feet above it. About a quarter of the space was taken up with the house's heating system, the pipes, vents and elephantine tubing of the water tank and furnace. There were boxes of household ephemera pushed into corners – ancient toys and broken domestic gadgetry, knick-knacks, mouldering comics, folders of Dev's teenage artwork and all the old ledger books, the pages curled and yellowed with age, from back when the father still had his taxi business. There was a thin mattress on a metal spring frame pushed along one wall and a desk bearing a big, boxy, dust-caked computer monitor, beneath the desk a hard drive the size of a suitcase and an intestinally knotted hank of plugs and cabling that no longer plugged into anything.

Irish houses tended to have attics, not basements. Dev's father had got the idea from American shows. One of the father's earliest and more benign flights of fancy. While it was being dug out, the father had had great plans for the basement – turning it into a games room, putting in a home gym or work bench – but by the time it was completed, his interest, as it so often did, had already receded elsewhere and the space became a repository for household junk, until little Dev turned it into his den. The bed dated from then, ditto the home computer and desk. Dev had spent much of his childhood in the basement, had often slept down here. Other kids went out. Dev went under the floorboards.

He came down the basement stairs, obliged to stoop as he made his way over to the bed. He tucked the sheet in under the mattress, neatly lining the edges, then the bedspread, set the pillow against the metal headboard.

He came back up into the kitchen and the Ferdias brought the kid down. Doll did not protest, just did as he was told. Dev took a seat at the kitchen table. Amid the shards of the shattered plate, Georgie had gulped down the remains of the rib sandwich and was now licking the grease spot on the floor. There were the sounds of talking coming from the basement, murky and not quite intelligible, the low, measured voice of Gabe punctuated by grunts, maybe from Sketch, maybe from the kid, maybe both. Then scraping and clunking sounds, like furniture was being shunted around. The Ferdias came back up.

'There a key?' Gabe asked.

Dev found the key in one of the drawers and gave it to Gabe. Gabe locked the door and pocketed the key.

'You're not a spirits man, are you?' he said to Dev, hunting through the overhead cupboards.

'Spirits?'

'Liquor. Whiskey, rum, that sort of – ah!'

Gabe pulled a bottle of Baileys from the back of one of the cupboards.

'That's the mother's,' Dev said.

'No doubt,' Gabe said. He unscrewed the cap and sniffed. 'You reckon poor old Moira would mind? It's just sitting there otherwise.'

Gabe poured three measures of Baileys, raised his glass.

'Here's to the English brothers,' he said.

The Baileys tasted sweet going down, then hit Dev in the chest as a slow, muffling warmth.

'I'm starved,' Gabe announced with a yawn. He fixed a bowl of Coco Pops for himself and Sketch. The Ferdias ate steadily, intently. Dev listened to the contented machinic crunching of their jaws and cast repeated glances towards the basement door. He kept expecting the kid to start hammering on the other side of it, demanding to be let out.

'How are you doing, Dev, are you shook?' Gabe said.

'I'm all right.'

'Didn't you think we were really going to do it?' Sketch said.

'Lift a young fella off the street?'

'We told you we were going to.'

And they had. A couple of months back, they had come over to Dev's gaff as they often did and spent the night sitting on Dev's sofa, drinking Dev's beers and giving out yards about that entitled little prick, Cillian English. That obstinate, cement-headed cunt, Cillian English. He owed Mulrooney money, a fair fucking pile of it, and he had owed it for far too long now; it was getting to the point, contended the Ferdias, where there needed to be consequences. English's kid brother and mother lived in town, and maybe what they needed to do was do something to *them*, to show Cillian neither they nor Mulrooney were fucking around. They could grab the brother and keep hold of him here, they said. Dev's gaff would be perfect, they said, and Dev remembers them going around and around in giddy circles about the logistics of it all, glorying in the idea that Cillian English would finally get what was coming to him.

Then they left at three in the morning, and Dev never heard another thing about it. Days went by, then weeks. Nothing happened and nothing continued to happen. When the Ferdias next appeared to drop off more sports bags of stuff, there wasn't word one about Cillian English or his family, and so Dev had quietly concluded that all the Ferdias had been doing that night was indulging a drunken fantasy of exaction before coming to their senses and forgetting all about it.

'How's this gonna work, though?' Dev asked. 'How long can you keep him here?'

Sketch smiled with wolfish satisfaction at Gabe.

'I knew this fella didn't believe us. He didn't think we had it in us.'

Dev pressed his tongue to the roof of his mouth. An after-tinge of creamy rancidity from the Baileys.

'I did think you were maybe just blowing a bit of shite,' he said. 'Just letting off steam on account of being so riled up by the English buck.'

'It's nothing to do with being riled up,' Gabe said, 'it's business.'

'The English buck riles me up,' Sketch admitted.

'But how's grabbing his kid brother going to help anything?' Dev said.

Gabe poured himself a second Baileys and drank it off. He took out a pack of cigarettes and lit one.

'Before we decided on this tack,' he said, 'myself and himself rocked up to English's gaff and right there in front of his lowing beoir bate seven shades of shit out of the man, and for a finish I stuck his hand in a drawer and Sketch roundhoused it until the drawer and the lad's hand were in absolute ribbons. We told him that if he didn't make good with Mulrooney pronto then the next time we saw him we'd be minded to fuck his entire carcass into the Moy.'

Gabe's smile, as he reminisced, was almost admiring.

'And did any of that make a blind bit of difference?' he said. 'That's the problem with the English buck. You can only threaten a man on the premise he gives enough of a fuck about his own skin to want to save it. So, if there's no merit in threatening him directly, you have to take another tack.'

He ashed the cigarette into the pool of pale brown milk in the bottom of his bowl. He looked at the basement door, bared his teeth and let slow spouts of smoke fall through them.

'If this doesn't get the English buck's attention, nothing will.'

The Ferdias flipped a coin. Sketch won. Dev showed him to the mother's room upstairs. In his own room, Dev swallowed a pill from the phial on the dresser next to his bed and went back downstairs while he waited for the grogginess to kick in.

In the hallway he righted the tipped-over coat stand, layering his mother's old coats back onto it. He went into the sitting room to retrieve his laptop. Gabe was on the sofa, smoke wreathing his head, drinking another beer and watching the TV with the sound off. On the screen shining-eyed people with stunned, disconnected smiles were being interviewed, talking rapidly into a microphone in the dark space of what looked like a nightclub, the pale, flashing limbs of the crowd jostling about them.

'What if he tries to get out?' Dev said.

'That's why I'm staying down here tonight.'

'There's stuff in the basement. Implements.'

'Implements?'

'Things he could try as a weapon.'

'What, like that big-arsed computer? I suppose he could drop it on your foot,' Gabe said. He looked at Dev.

'Don't worry about that young fella,' he said. 'That young fella is going to do as he's told. We wouldn't have got him this far if he wasn't going to do as he was told.'

In the kitchen Dev poured himself a bowl of Coco Pops and ate them alone at the table, chewing carefully and pausing whenever he thought he heard a noise coming from the basement; on each occasion he held his breath, a mouthful of mulched cereal hanging in his arrested jaws, and stared at the door until he was sure he had not.

He could not believe there was a person down there.

He wondered if the Ferdias had tied him up. Or scared him. Or hurt him. He imagined himself returning to the sitting room and demanding the key from Gabe, tearing open the basement door and telling the kid to beat it off out the road.

He kept eating his Coco Pops.

The house had gone quiet. Georgie had settled in his basket by the back door and resumed snoozing.

Though he knew it made no sense – because it was the middle of the night and only a few hours had elapsed since the Ferdias had grabbed the kid, and even if someone had witnessed that event and immediately alerted the police, and the police had in turn immediately alerted the press, there was no way they would have a story out already – Dev nonetheless scoured the websites of all the local and regional papers, to confirm there was as yet no mention of a missing kid.

When he was satisfied there was nothing, he looked up POMERANIAN JACK RUSSELL BAD LUNGS and POMERANIAN JACK RUSSELL BREATH-ING PROBLEMS. He found several posts warning of the susceptibility of such mixes to poorliness, but even more posts insisting on the exact opposite, that such cross-breeds were a deceptively hardy and resilient dog. As he continued to scroll, Georgie came up out of his basket and began pacing back and forth by Dev's foot, emitting the hoarse, pleading whine which meant he needed to go to the toilet. Dev needed to piss too. He closed the laptop, yawned and rubbed at his face. He could feel the pill work-ing its sedating magic, calming his blood and thickening his thoughts, making them slow and settle like silt at the bottom of his darkening mind.

He let the dog out the back door. The rain had stopped. The night air had that clean, stony smell it got after rain. Georgie trotted down the garden and Dev followed. The garden was big and empty, bordered by a concrete wall, invisible now in the dark. Dev trudged a good ways out into the grass. There was no dark like country dark, the blackness beyond the house so total that looking out across the back fields he could not tell where the earth ended and the sky began. All was void. At the bottom of the garden he turned back and faced the house. The lone burning rectangle of the kitchen window cast an apron of illumination a little way out onto the grass, but Dev was stood well beyond the reach of its glow. He took out his prick. He could hear Georgie nearby, truffling in the grass, divining his own spot in which to urinate. As he pissed, he tilted his head all the way back and looked straight up. There, in the furthest, purest reaches of the sky, the stars grew in distinctness and brightness until it felt like he could reach out and touch the cold phosphorescent centres of them. The arc of his warm stream wavered and guttered out. He shook himself off and zipped up.

He stood there for a while, knowing there was nowhere to go but back into the house.

'We're in the shit now, Georgie,' he said into the dark.

2

Nicky Hennigan was sat in her car in the drive of the English house, waiting on Doll and Doll's mam, Sheila. She was the other side of an eight-hour shift in the bar of the Pearl Hotel, bone-tired after a week of such shifts, and was content, just now, to do nothing but chew on the plastic cap of her hoodie's drawstring and gaze mindlessly into the driveway hedge. There, embedded deep in the hedge's ordered crush of spiky privet, she saw what she always saw: the three-quarters hidden, shrivelled grey panels of an ancient Umbro football. Nicky had been going out with Doll English for coming on two years, and that ball had been stuck in there every bit as long. She wondered how much longer she would have to look at it.

The front door clattered on its hinges and Doll came shaping down the lawn to the drive. He rapped a knuckle against the window and she winced, let the hoodie's cap drop from her mouth and rolled down the glass.

'Let me drive us in,' Doll said.

'You can drive us in when you've a licence entitles you to,' Nicky said.

Doll tutted in mock exasperation and came around to the passenger side. He climbed in and leaned across the handbrake to kiss her, smelling powerfully of aftershave and weed. Nicky turned her face so his lips caught her cheek. If Doll noticed the turn, he did not let on. He flipped down the sun visor above his head and made an excruciated expression – jaws clenched and teeth bared – into the little rectangle of the visor mirror. He lifted his chin and tilted it this way and that, appraising the dotted nap of his neck, and let out a low, impressed whistle. This pantomime of vanity, Nicky knew, was intended to rise her.

'Loves himself, I'd say,' Nicky said, taking the rise.

'Somebody has to,' Doll said.

'Where's that mother of yours?' Nicky said, eyeing the front door of the house.

'You know she gets wound up before these meetings.' Doll dipped his head and with the tips of his fingers did something flicky and indiscernible to his fringe.

Nicky stifled a yawn and her eyes filmed. The hedge blurred. She blinked until it was clear again.

'How long's that ball been stuck in there?' she said.

'Hnh?' Doll grunted.

'Every time I'm sat here waiting on you, I'm looking at that ball stuck in there.'

'Ah,' he said, 'that's been there forever. Cillian fucked that ball at my head when I was, like, five and it got stuck in there.'

'That ball's been stuck in there since you were five?'

Doll studied the hedge in seeming consideration, the wilted ball hanging there like a jawless skull.

'It's burst,' he said, 'it's no use.'

'It'd drive me mad having to look at it every day.'

'In fairness,' he said, 'I'm only noticing it now because you said it. The rest of the time, it's like I don't see it.'

'Every day, the same spot, it's stuck right there. How would you not see it?' Nicky insisted.

'I'm seeing it now,' Doll said defensively.

The door to the house clattered again and out came Sheila English. She was a small, slight woman but did not seem so when she was on the move. She was wearing dark glasses and a navy-and-white Reebok tracksuit Nicky was pretty sure had at one point belonged to Doll. Sheila marched straight around to her son's side of the car.

'Come out,' she ordered.

Doll tutted again but quickly got out, shunted forward the passenger seat and clambered into the back of the car.

'There she is, now,' Sheila said, sliding in next to Nicky. 'You're just out of work, love?'

Under her hoodie, Nicky was wearing a grey shirt with *The Pearl Hotel Bar & Restaurant* embroidered over the breast pocket, grey trousers and black runners.

'Just out now, yeah.'

'You'll be flat out with the festival this weekend.'

'There's a rake of bookings in the hotel, all right,' Nicky said. 'After tonight I'm working straight through to Monday.'

'God love you, girl, you never stop,' Sheila said, 'and you're very good to run me into town on top of it all.'

'Isn't it on the way, Sheila?' Nicky said as she started the car and put it into gear.

Sheila and Doll lived on the Killala road, several miles outside of Ballina town. The sun was glinting brittlely in a sky of grey cloud as they passed the grounds of the old Killala Bay Hotel, shuttered years ago. On the tennis courts out front the nets were still strung up, the sagging mesh as frayed as used dental floss. Then came low hills and a wide, flat interval of bogland. In the fields there were dark arteries of turf visible where long channels had been dug out of the bog. A car and a utility trailer were parked down one of the lanes, a dog resting on all fours on the car's bonnet watching a man and a child dismantle stacks of footed turf and toss the blunt clods into the trailer. The child was wearing Marigold gloves, yellow as the gorse ignited in spiky clusters out along the hills. Then the bog was gone and they entered the town limits. Houses and commercial buildings multiplied along the roadside. They passed Faughnan's car dealership, an Applegreen's petrol station with a sit-in Supermac's, a truck depot, the barriered road into a commercial estate built just along the edge of Belleek Wood.

'How's that brother of yours?' Sheila said.

'Connor's flat out as usual,' Nicky said.

'Of course he is. Where is he now, England?'

'Last time I heard from him he was in, uh, Groningen. That was a couple of days back.'

Connor was Nicky's older brother. He was twenty-five. He had been Nicky's legal guardian for the last six years, ever since the deaths of their parents. For the last couple of years Connor had been driving trucks for a haulage company and often spent long weeks out on the road all over the UK and Europe. When Connor was away, like now, Nicky preferred to be out and in the world, no matter how tired and tetchy she was. They lived in an apartment together on the other side of town but the place could be hard to take when it was just herself.

'Groningen,' Sheila said. 'That's where, now? Belgium?'

'That'd be Holland, Mother,' Doll piped up.

'Apologies the geography's not up to muster, but fair play to Connor, he's doing his best. It's certain other specimens,' Sheila said, 'I find suffer from a lack of gusto.'

'My gusto's grand,' Doll said. 'I'm packed to the gills with gusto.'

'You're packed to the gills with something.'

'You know you look like a police informant in them glasses.'

'The glasses are compulsory,' Sheila said, touching the frames and adjusting them. 'I can do nothing about the glasses, I'm afraid.'

'Head still at you these days?' Nicky said, though she knew well what the answer would be. The glasses Sheila wore were prescription. She suffered from a sensitivity to light. Too much light, direct light, light above a certain intensity, brought on migraines.

'I had to take a beta blocker before I came out, because I could feel a little bit of a thing brewing there in the back of the head,' Sheila said. 'I've started noticing a kind of aura just before it comes on.'

'An aura?' Nicky said.

'It's a recent development,' Sheila said. 'The air takes on a quality. A haziness, a kind of glow comes over things. If I look at a light, for example, it starts to dim and then brighten, like someone's messing with the dial. That's the early-warning system kicking in. That's how I know there's a migraine in the post. The aura comes over me.'

'There's an awful mystical bent to Mother's suffering these days,' Doll said.

'More unsolicited tuppencing from the back,' Sheila said. 'Does he ever be at that with you, Nicky? Providing a running commentary on every word that comes out of your mouth.'

'He knows better than to try that with me,' Nicky said.

'What's the plan tonight?' Sheila said.

'I don't know, we might watch the fireworks, I reckon,' Doll said.

'The fireworks and what else?'

'Cannon's having a few people over to his. Reckon we'll drop in there.'

'The Cannon place. How many is a few?'

'Now that I don't know, Mother. Nicky might do a headcount if you ask nicely.'

'Very smart. You're at ours tonight, Nicky?'

'She is, yeah,' Doll said.

'I'm just asking,' Sheila said. 'Nicky knows she's always welcome.'

'I do, Sheila,' Nicky said, but Sheila's attention was already locked back on her son.

'I know you're going to meet that brother of yours and don't say otherwise,' Sheila said.

'Why would I say otherwise?' Doll said.

'Electing to leave that detail out.'

'I didn't leave it out. I didn't think it was worth mentioning,' Doll said. 'But yeah, I might well drop in to Cillian's. Why wouldn't I?'

'There's no law forbids it.'

'You could always forbid me.'

'I could, only you'd be twice as enticed to be spending time with that man in his milieu if I did.'

'His milieu!' Doll scoffed.

'I know the sorts that do be congregating over there. That house is a wild house.'

'Cillian's a grown man,' Doll said, 'he can have who he wants over to his gaff.'

'And that woman letting him have the run of the place,' Sheila said, meaning Sara Duane, Cillian's girlfriend. 'You think she'd have more sense.'

'Not everyone is a bastion of sense like yourself, Mother.'

'I don't know how she puts up with him,' Sheila grumbled, 'but then some people have temperaments you can't legislate for. That job of hers, for instance, I don't know how she does it; looking into people's mouths all day. It'd do something to you.'

'She's an assistant though?' Nicky said. She knew Sara worked in a dental practice in town. 'She's not doing the actual dentistry.'

'The assistants have to rinse out your mouth with those

little jets,' Sheila said, 'they have to clean off the instruments. Thank you, but I'd rather pick sweetcorn out of baby shit for a living.'

'There's little in the way of congregating happening in that house these days,' Doll said. 'Cillian's been keeping it low-key.'

'Has he now?' Sheila said.

'He has, yeah,' Doll said. 'All you've to do is drop over any time and see.'

'Mmh,' Sheila grunted, and turned her attention to the town sliding past her window. They were in Ballina proper now. Nicky took them through the tiny roundabout at Dunnes Stores and on up Main Street. On Main Street they joined a small tailback, and moved in fits and starts past pubs and franchise coffee places, the AIB branch and the hangdog frontage of local businesses on their last legs – MACKIN TAILORS, BURKES SHOES, CUDDY'S NEWSAGENT & PHARMACY. The town was busier than usual for a Friday afternoon, which was to be expected. The Salmon Festival, an annual week-long celebration and the biggest local event of the year, was officially kicking off with a fireworks display on the quays later that night, though the festivities had already informally begun; along the pavement and in the alleys off the main thoroughfare there were rows of stalls assembled with their wares on display, and the canvas awnings and frames of more stalls going up. Nicky saw vines of cured sausage, wheels and wedges of cheese, tarts in tin trays, knitwear, jars of compote, local-ish IPAs. Teenagers and young families milled. Groups of young men, on it early, languished in the doorways of pubs, supping beer in plastic cups and peering out into the bright commotion of the street with glazed, red-cheeked smiles of innocent connivance, arms folded farmerishly across their chests even as they leaned in close to speak out of the side of their mouths and provoke each other into voluminous spasms of quiet, sly laughter.

'Now, Nicky,' Sheila said, turning away from the window, 'don't be letting this fella keep you out until all hours. You've been working today. You look tired.'

'Cheers,' Nicky said.

'Oh, you know what I mean!' Sheila said. 'You're a gorgeous girl, but it's OK to look tired if you're tired.'

'Don't worry about Nicky, Mother,' Doll said, 'she doesn't do nothing she doesn't want to.'

'From what I can see she spends a great deal of time chauffeuring you around, and then the poor girl ends up having to drive me around into the bargain, not activities that could be too high up anyone's list of things they might actually want to do.'

'It's no bother, Sheila,' Nicky said. Every time she gave Sheila a lift, they went through a version of this ritual; Sheila lamenting how much of an imposition she was, which in turn obliged Nicky to insist that she was not.

'Look at this pair,' Doll said, leaning between the front seats to get a better view.

In front of the Silver Lantern Chinese takeaway there was a tall, skinny lad with a goatee in a battered leather jacket covered in psychedelic spatters of paint working his way through a tin tray of curry chips, one hand trailing a length of rope loosely noosed around the neck of the goat standing next to him. The goat had glowing yellow eyes. Its horns were knobbled sickles curving back out of its small white skull.

'Thought it was just dogs took after their owners.'

The man and the goat did share similarly long-boned, bewhiskered faces.

'The element this festival brings in,' Sheila said.

'The festival's good craic,' Doll said.

'And who'll be cleaning up that animal's shite when it scutters all over the street?'

'Not me and not you, Mother.'

Nicky turned off Main Street and took them up Convent Hill, past the grounds of the girls' secondary school. When they reached the district hospital, they drove by a row of small bungalows all painted in the same dingy institutional whitewash. These buildings were known locally as the Units. They were residential homes for people in long-term psychiatric care. Beyond the Units was a large two-storey building. Various offices occupied the upper levels of the building. A treatment clinic was run out of the basement and various support groups, including a counselling group for family members of alcoholics. This was where Nicky was dropping Sheila. Sheila went to these meetings, not very often, maybe only every three months or so, and had been doing so ever since Doll and Cillian's father, Vincie, had left them and left the country.

Sheila was bent close to the window, scrutinising the footpath leading up to the clinic. There was no one else around but a man sitting on the upper steps of the building, smoking a cigarette. Nicky could sense him watching as she parked the car.

'I wonder if there'll even be anyone at this tonight, with the festival and all,' Sheila said.

'Go on now if you're going, Mother,' Doll said.

Sheila looked at Doll, frowned like she was about to say something, then checked herself and gently shook her head.

'Police informant,' she muttered, and opened the door.

'Good luck with it now,' Nicky said.

Sheila got out of the car and the man on the steps lifted his hand an expectant fraction, cigarette crooked between his fingers, ready to salute her if she decided to look his way. She did not. Her small, purposeful form went right down the lower steps of the building and in through the basement door.

'She is as wound up,' Nicky said.

'I told you,' Doll said.

Nicky heard the *tchk* of a lighter and a plume of smoke jellyfished over her shoulder. She turned to see Doll puffing intently on the stub of a half-gone joint, its revived cherry dimming and glowing, like he was giving it CPR.

'It's not going to catch,' Nicky said.

'Patience now,' Doll said through clenched teeth as he puffed and puffed and the cherry flared and finally held steady.

'Back from the brink,' he said.

Nicky glanced again at the steps Sheila had disappeared down.

'Why does she go to those meetings if they wind her up?'

Doll screwed his eyes against the smoke.

'I don't know,' he said. 'It's stirring shit up. You wouldn't do it unless you wanted to. Like picking at a scab.'

'I don't want to pick at scabs, but I do it anyway,' Nicky said, gesturing for the joint.

'That's what I mean,' Doll said.

'That's cutting now,' Nicky said as she took a drag and the smoke burned in her throat, 'there's barely the one hit left in it.'

'Finish it.'

Nicky took a last drag and flicked the joint out her window as Doll slid forward the front seat, stepped out of the car and got back in next to her. He slammed the door after him and the report of it seemed to activate the man on the steps, who rose to his feet, flicked away his own cigarette, and began making his way towards the car.

'Who's this prick now?' Doll complained.

The man, now that he was upright, was very tall. He looked to be in his fifties, bald on top with a chalky stubble of grey hair running around his head. He was wearing a roomy sports jacket over a T-shirt, brown corduroys that did not match the jacket, a pair of pulverised tennis shoes with loosely knotted laces the colour of a rat's tail. When he got to the car he squinted in through the windscreen at Nicky, then Doll, walked around to Doll's side of the car and stood there, waiting, until Doll rolled down his window.

'You all right?' Doll said.

'Yes,' the man said. 'I can indeed.'

'Can what?'

'Now I'm up close I can see you've an awful resemblance to someone. Was that your mother just went in there?'

'It was, yeah.'

'I have to say I don't recognise that lady. But I do know the head on you. Any money I know your father, only I need a hint. What's your name?'

'My name?' Doll said.

'If you don't mind.'

Doll looked dubiously across at Nicky and back at the man.

'Donal,' he said.

'Donal what?'

'English.'

'Well, there you go!' the man said brightly. 'Vincie English would be your father.'

'Yeah.'

'I knew Vincie English back in the day. Not well now, but you only had to be in his vicinity to know he was there. But he's headed for the hills now, isn't he?'

'He's been gone for a while,' Doll admitted.

'He used to call me Sergeant any time he wound up in the back of my taxi.'

'Sergeant?'

'I used to run a taxi around town, and before I ran the taxi I was in the Guards. I never got next nor near the rank of Sergeant but that's what Vincie called me anyway. Jesus, but he was some demon for the drink,' the man said with a shake of his head. 'I used to be out at all hours with the taxi, and one night I was parked down the alley next to the Tesco, taking a sleep in the back seat, the way I did between calls. It must have been four in the morning. I woke up with an almighty urge to – excuse me – piddle, so I stepped out and did the business against the alley wall. When I went to get back in the car, didn't I only get the fright of my life. What did I see but the body of a full-grown man wedged in under my front wheels. For a second, I thought Oh Jesus, I somehow let the handbrake off in my sleep and managed to run over some poor bastard, but then I realised the fella under the wheels was snoring. It was Vincie, tucked in under the engine to keep himself warm I suppose, the way a stray cat would be. My Lord! Lucky for him nature called because otherwise I would have climbed straight in the front of the car none the wiser and surely rolled right over him. He stunk of drink and when I went to wake him the man got as indignant at me, like I'd broken into his house and was trying to rout him out of his own bed.'

'Well, that's something,' Doll said flatly.

'It's beyond calculation,' the man said. 'And where did you say he went?'

'I didn't,' Doll said. Nicky saw his jaw go taut. 'He's abroad in a place called Calgary.'

'Where's that?'

'Canada.'

'What's it like?'

'I don't know.'

'You never been?'

'Nah.'

'How long's he been out there?'

'He's been gone a while.'

'How long is a while?'

'I don't know. Five years.'

'Five years and you've not been out to him?'

'Never got the invite.'

'And what on earth brought him out there?'

'He was out there in the eighties, working on the oilfields.'

'And that's what he's at now?'

'I don't know what he's at now,' Doll said. 'Drinking like a demon, presumably.'

'Hah,' the man scoffed gently and almost contritely, now that his curiosity had been satisfied.

'You're going to be late if you're heading in there,' Doll said, nodding towards the basement steps.

'Oh, that's nothing to do with me,' the man said. 'I live here.'

'What's that mean?' Doll said.

'He means he lives in the Units,' Nicky said.

The man tilted his head to get a better look at Nicky.

'The young one is right,' he said. 'I'm shacked up in here with the poor creatures do talk to God.'

'Oh,' Doll said. Nicky saw a smile of relieved insolence creep up Doll's face.

'The creatures who *hear* God, I should say,' the man continued. 'There's nothing wrong with talking *to* God. That's just pleading your case into the air and there's no harm in that, lots of people do that, my own mother used to do that. The trouble begins when God starts talking back.'

'That'd be the trouble all right,' Doll agreed brightly.

'It's not anyone's fault. A mind can only work with the signals it receives, do you know? As opposed to the noise. The calculations made on its behalf. This lady here knows what I'm talking about.'

'She would,' Doll said, 'she's all about the signals she receives.'

Nicky was thinking. Something about the combination of professions the man had just cited – Guard, taximan – had rung a bell. She remembered a story that went around years ago about a taximan who used to be a Guard. There had been an incident, involving a woman. The woman had been a teacher in Muredach's, back when Cillian would have been a student. She had been kidnapped, attacked, something awful like that.

'Donal English,' the man continued. 'I saw you sitting here and I thought, I *know* I know this buck's head.'

The man took out his wallet and produced a couple of notes.

'Will you do something for me, young English? You know the bookies there on Main Street next door to Horan's pub. There's a dog running in the 8.15 in Clonmel tonight. I want you to go in and put twenty euros on it.'

'On a dog,' Doll said.

'Tell them it's for Martin Hendrick,' the man said, reaching in through the window and pushing the notes into Doll's hand. 'They know me. They know I do send people in on my behalf sometimes. The dog is Perilous Endeavour. She's running in the 8.15 at Clonmel. Odds are one to seven. At the desk they'll hand you a slip. You hand the slip right back to them and tell them hold it under my name.

Martin Hendrick. *Sergeant* Martin Hendrick, as poor old Vincie would say.'

'Why don't you just go down yourself?'

'Oh, I could,' Hendrick said, 'but there's activities they frown on in here. Not that you're *not* allowed to do them, exactly, but they *are* frowned upon. And however discreet you try and go about your business in town, word has a way of creeping back here.'

Doll looked helplessly at the notes in his hand.

'You gave me twenty-five,' he said.

'The five is your handling fee.'

'What if I just pocket the lot and you never see me again.'

'If you do, you do.'

'Look, man, I don't have time for this.'

Doll tried to hand back the money, but Hendrick stepped away from the window.

'It'll take you two minutes,' he said.

Doll looked at Nicky, back at the money, then clucked his tongue in unhappy resignation.

'I'm telling you I don't have time, man, so don't blame me if you go down there later and they tell you this bet never got placed.'

'Perilous Endeavour,' Hendrick said with a smile. '8.15.'

Nicky and Doll sat in silence and watched Hendrick cut an unhurried diagonal across the little green and then let himself inside the door of one of the bungalows, ducking his head on the way in.

Nicky started the car and took them back down past the Units, towards the exit.

Doll burst out laughing.

'What the fuck was that?' he said.

'I don't know,' Nicky said.

'Tell me you saw that fella too. Tell me I wasn't just hallucinating.'

'He was real.'

Doll fluttered the notes in his hand.

'I have his money, so he must be real. Did that man really just ask me to put a bet on for him?'

'You told him not to,' Nicky said. 'You told him you wouldn't do it.'

'And then bringing up my father. He's lucky I didn't get out of the car and lace him out of it when he started up with his little anecdote.'

'The man's in an institution. I wouldn't put too much stock in anything he has to say.'

'Going on about my oul fella when he's the one living in the mental. Did you see what he was wearing? Any money all that gear was Vincent de Paul's, and no belt on the trousers. The zip was flying low, too. I thought we were going to get a show any second.'

'Will you stop?' Nicky smiled.

Doll waved the notes again.

'All that cracked oul prick really wanted was to get a bet on.'

They were waiting on a light at the Main Street junction. Next to what had once been a record shop, a man in a smutched apron was cooking burgers and sausages on a barbecue cart rigged up to look like an old-time steam train, smoke swirling in bright white gouts out of the cart's chimney spout. A child gulped Coke from a can as red as an apple. A stilt walker in a rumpled suit and an oversized papier-mâché mask fashioned to resemble the craggy features of an old man and wielding a papier-mâché pint of Guinness the size of a violin case, tottered spiderishly down the street in a pantomime of drunkenness.

The light went green and Nicky turned back down Main Street.

'The creatures that do talk to God,' Doll said. 'Is that how he put it?'

'That was it, I think,' Nicky said.

'Talk about mystical,' Doll said.

As Nicky brought them down Main Street Doll watched the row of cars parked along the kerb.

'Here, pull in,' he said.

'What?'

'There's a space,' Doll said, 'pull in until I do that prick his favour.'

Nicky saw the entrance to Horan's pub, and a couple of doors down, the bookies. She pulled into the space Doll had indicated. He shot her a scornful and apologetic look before he jumped out of the car and darted into the doorway of the bookies. Nicky sat there with the engine running. The stilt walker had followed them down along Main Street and Nicky watched the elongated figure approach and then feint towards a group of pedestrians, as if it was about to career right into them, and at the last moment veer back into the middle of the footpath and continue clicking its way down the street.

3

B Y ALL accounts, Cillian English had been a terror as a young fella. Fights, thieving, drink and drugs, any amount of skipping school until the school threw him out. When he was seventeen, he stole a car and rear-ended an ice-cream truck parked in the owner's driveway at two in the morning. The crash was deliberate and retaliatory; a week earlier, the ice-cream man had refused to serve an extremely stoned Cillian and a couple of his equally intoxi-cated mates after they had inadvertently wandered into the midst of a children's birthday party in the park at which the ice-cream man was handing out 99s to the kids. The other two lads got away, but Cillian's airbag failed to deploy and he broke his collarbone on the steering wheel, and had to wait curled up in agony on the ice-cream man's lawn while the bewildered and pyjama-clad ice-cream man and his wife took turns berating him until the cops showed up. Cillian received a suspended sentence and was sent to rehab. The stint in rehab introduced him to an elevated calibre of delinquent and inspired him to change his ways in the sense that, once he was out, he went from recreationally abusing drugs to selling them. By the time his father left, Cillian was an established local dealer, increasingly brazen enough in his activities that Sheila was soon unable to handle him. She told him if he wasn't going to quit selling drugs, he had to get out of the house. So he did.

Cillian had been twenty-two at that stage. Sara Duane was ten years older than him. She had the house in Glen Gardens from a broken marriage to a philandering grocer, a solid job, and on the weekends she liked to get high. Cillian was her dealer. Though at that point they were apparently not romantically involved, Cillian, with the opportunist's nose for a latent advantage, showed up on her doorstep and said he needed a place to crash for a couple of days. Three years later and he was still there.

Glen Gardens had gone up in the early 2000s, a quartet of horseshoe-shaped cul-de-sacs of semi-detached one-storey houses that all looked the exact same. It was a well-to-do estate, the other residents mostly young families with people carriers parked out front. Sara's place was at the end of one of the cul-de-sacs.

Once Cillian moved in, he started dealing right out of the house. His customers came over to buy and then they hung around and smoked and snorted half of what they had bought and then they bought more to make up the shortfall. Nicky was going out with Doll by then and got to experience the house first-hand. The atmosphere was that of a continuous, continuously improvised party that periodically doldrumed and never ended, contending playlists emanating from different rooms, a standing bank of smoke shimmering in seeming permanence in the sitting room, pin-eyed young ones rattling on the front door at all hours. And things had gone on that way until a year or so ago, when Cillian suddenly stopped dealing. With the drugs gone, Cillian's customers went away too. What Doll had told his mother was true; Sara and Cillian's house was no longer a wild house.

It was Sara answered the door.

'There's the two,' she said with a slightly frazzled air. Her hair, ice blonde with long black roots, was up in a bun, and she was still in her blue work scrubs. She smelled like chemicals. 'Sorry, I'm just in myself.'

'Where's the fiend?' Doll said.

'Sleeping Beauty's in the sitting room,' Sara said.

Doll touched open the sitting-room door and Nicky followed him in. The curtains were drawn, the TV off. Cillian was sitting slumped on the sofa with his arms folded and his head dropped onto his chest, a seashell ashtray resting on his knee with a dead joint in it. He was densely asleep, the only noise in the room the snores escaping from his nose in jagged combustive pops, like logs spitting in a fire.

'Cillian,' Doll said.

Cillian's shoulders jerked and his head shot up. The ashtray jumped on his knee but did not fall.

'Yup,' he muttered, looking blinkingly about in the gloom until he saw Doll and Nicky.

'Well,' he said.

'You look out of it, man,' Doll said.

'I *am* out of it.'

He smiled and coughed, cleared his throat and wiped at

his face. He was pale and unshaven, his greasy hair pushed disorderedly back from his brow, like he'd been running his hand constantly through it. Tints the pale blue of cue-chalk scooped the lower orbits of his eyes.

'Conked out here in the middle of the day then he can't sleep at night,' Sara said from the doorway.

'You're as bad as Mother now,' Doll said.

'Don't be telling me that,' Cillian said. 'Mother and her ailments. How is that woman?'

'Just dropped her into a meeting.'

'She still at that?'

'Of course she is.'

'Fair play to her.'

'She was fretting about me coming over here.'

'Was she now,' Cillian said. He coughed and cleared his throat again, transferred the ashtray from his knee to the end table, brushed down the worn denim of his jeans and sat up. 'I hope you told her I'm as good as gold these days.'

'I told her she should come see for herself.'

'How'd that suggestion go down?'

'Oh, you know.'

'I do,' Cillian said. 'Come in, sit down.'

There was a duvet balled up on the sofa.

'Someone been kipping here?' Doll said, gathering up the duvet and looking to Cillian to see where he should dispose of it.

'Here,' Cillian said, 'just fuck it on the ground there.'

Doll did as he was told.

'The council,' Cillian groaned, running his hand through his hair and grinding the heel of his palm into his eye sockets. 'The council moved a street lamp down the street, put it right in front of our bedroom window. No matter how tight I get the window slats, this tenacious fucking beam of light manages to worm its way through the gaps and keep at me all night long. So. I kip down here, sometimes.'

'Tell them move it again,' Doll suggested.

'I should put it out with a brick is what I should do.'

Doll took a seat on the sofa and Nicky joined him.

'How's Hennigan?' Cillian said to her.

'I'm all right,' she said.

The room did not smell great, and Cillian looked even more dishevelled than the last time they had been here. On the coffee table was a bowl of milk in which a few pale Rice Krispies floated like grubs, a scatter of Rizla papers, a Ziploc bag of weed, a brown phial of pills and something Nicky had not seen before: a large, shallow glass bowl. The bowl was filled with a pale mound of sand on which were arranged three small, jagged rocks, a dark green plant with spiky tendrils, a swatch of moss and a small wooden rake.

She sat forward, picked up the rake and combed a length of the sand.

'Zen rock garden,' Cillian said. 'Game changer.'

'Is it?' Nicky said.

'Herself picked it up for me a few weeks ago. Before that, I was going through this black spell,' he said, 'just sitting here every day, staring at the wall grinding my teeth and fantasising about putting a bolt through the skull. Now whenever the head gets at me, I pick up that rake and start making little shapes in the sand and it just' – he raised his hand and held it horizontal in the air – 'it levels me right out.'

'Really?' Nicky said.

'Swear to God.'

'A bolt through the skull,' Sara said. 'What am I meant to do with that?'

'It's ideation, you don't have to do nothing with it, the same as me,' Cillian said. 'When'd you get home?'

'Two minutes before they got here,' Sara said. 'How long were you asleep?'

'Never mind how long I was asleep,' Cillian said, 'we have guests, go on and fix us up some drinks.'

'You can fix your own fucking drinks,' Sara said, folding her arms.

'Ah, go on,' Cillian said in a wheedling tone that was both a parody of a plea and a genuine one.

Sara rolled her eyes, tutted, and headed off down the hall.

Cillian took out his phone and frowned at it. Nicky could see the cockeyed slant to his shoulders from the old collarbone break, and she remembered that the last time they were here, he'd had a cast on his arm. He'd broken the wrist and all the fingers on his right hand in some kind of fall, so he said. The cast was off now but she could see that he was still favouring his left hand.

'You know that woman never reaches out to me,' Cillian said. 'Never calls or texts. It's always me reaching out to her. And even then, in terms of her responding, she's awful patchy.'

'You know she's not great with the phone stuff,' Doll said.

'She has a way of making it seem like you're the one neglecting her though, like you're the one not making an effort.'

'But you don't make an effort.'

'I make an effort.'

'Show me your phone.'

'Why.'

'When was the last time you called her?'

'It's not exactly an inducement, knowing your own mother doesn't want to talk to you,' Cillian said.

'Of course she wants to talk to you,' Doll said.

'I text her,' Cillian said, 'I'll send a "how are you?" and I'll hear nothing for the guts of a week and right when I'm convinced that that's it so, she's finally cut the cord, I'll get back "I'm grand". Then not a word until I text her again. I'm following her lead, kid, I'm keeping exactly the distance she wants me to.'

'The pair of you do my head in,' Doll said with a shake of his head.

Sara returned to the room bearing a tray of glasses filled with Coca-Cola. Nicky took a sip and the scouring zap of whiskey burned up through her sinuses.

'That's strong,' she said.

'Duane's as heavy-handed with the measures,' Cillian said.

'Too strong?' Sara said.

'You're grand,' Nicky said.

'How are you, anyway?' Sara said, taking the chair next to Nicky's end of the sofa.

'I'm OK—' Nicky began.

'Met a man today knew the oul fella,' Doll said, turning to Nicky. 'What was his name again?'

Nicky waited a moment to see if it would click with Doll that he had cut across her, but he only kept looking at her, oblivious and expectant.

'Hendrick,' she said.

'Martin Hendrick,' Doll said to Cillian. 'You know that cunt?'

'Rings a vague bell,' Cillian said.

'Said he used to run taxis,' Doll said. 'Said he found the oul fella sleeping under the wheels of the taxi one night. Said he almost ran right over him.'

'Pity he didn't,' Cillian grinned.

'The funny thing is that this fella, Hendrick, he's living there in the hospital, in the Units,' Doll said.

'Living there?'

'Had me put a bet on the dogs for him in town and everything,' Doll said.

Nicky took a drink of her drink.

'You know him, actually,' she said to Cillian.

'Yeah?' Cillian said.

'Before he drove taxis he was a Guard,' Nicky said. 'He was the fella did something to that teacher you had. The one you all fancied who moved away.'

'Miss Lacey,' Cillian said. 'She taught German. Now there was a beoir.'

'I remember that,' Sara said, 'I remember that woman.'

'What was the story there again?' Doll said.

'What happened was one night your one Lacey came tripping out of Murphy's or Kennedy's, some pub down the town,' Cillian said. 'She was on her own, so she does the sensible thing and flags down a taxi, only the taximan who picks her up, instead of taking her home, he tears off out towards Luisbergh with her.'

'He took her to the silver strand,' Nicky said.

'Bombing it out there going ninety and talking a mile a minute about how there was something in the water he needed her to see. A spaceship that had fallen out of the sky. He'd seen it come right down over the strand, this big shining disc in flames, so he said. The story goes that as soon as they got to the strand, your man jumped out of the taxi and beelined straight for the water, shouting at her to come in with him. Lacey had her phone with her and was able to call the emergency. When the Guards got there your man was hypothermic and half drowned, getting ragdolled around in the Atlantic in the middle of the night.'

'You'd be out of your mind with fright,' Sara said.

'Rachel Lacey,' Cillian said. '*Racy Lacey* we used to call her. Every last lad was in love with her.'

'And that's the man decided to come sneer in my face about the oul fella,' Doll said.

'Sleeping under cars,' Cillian said. 'That's a new one on me, now.'

'He'd have been well capable of it,' Doll said.

'Remember Friday nights he'd come in absolutely pole-axed with the drink and go straight to bed and pass out?' Cillian said. 'He was working for Georgie Dockery on the sites and Dockery would pay all the boys in cash. By the time he got home, he'd half the pay packet sprayed up the jacks wall of whatever pub he'd been in and the rest was being held hostage in the wallet.'

Doll slumped back into the couch.

'I remember,' he said.

'The mother would do it herself sometimes,' Cillian continued. He was looking at Nicky as he spoke. 'Crawl in on her hands and knees and creep up to the side of the bed and fish the wallet out of your man's trousers trying not to wake him, but more often than not she'd send Doll in. He was only seven or eight at the time, the littlest of us, the lightest on his feet. He'd be in and out like a shot, nimble as a monkey. The mother would subtract whatever money she needed for the shopping and bills for the week and back into the oul fella's pocket the wallet would go.'

'He never noticed the money missing?' Nicky said.

'Probably just figured he drank it with the rest.'

'Sometimes, when I was right up next to him in the dark, the way he was breathing and all that, I was convinced he was awake,' Doll said, 'that he knew I was there and was just putting on that he was asleep.'

'You'd put nothing past him,' Cillian said.

He took a drink and a satisfied hiss escaped his clenched teeth. He looked at Nicky and smiled.

'No offence, Hennigan,' he said, 'but I reckon that in one way your parents done you a favour dying on you the way they did. A perfectly decent mammy and daddy by all accounts, both getting cancer like that, that's just brutal bad luck and nobody's fault, but on the upside you and the brother were left with nothing but good memories and everyone having to be respectful and sorry to you about it forever after.'

Nicky felt her insides pull tight like a wire.

'Yeah, we got fierce lucky,' she said.

'Cillian,' Doll said.

'That's an awful fucking ignorant thing to say,' Sara said, coming up out of her seat. There was the glare of tears in her eyes, and she looked like she might pitch her drink in Cillian's face, only her glass was already empty.

'I am ignorant!' Cillian said. 'You'll never hear me claim I'm not. I'm sorry now if that was insensitive of me, Nicky.'

'Don't worry about it,' Nicky said.

What else could she say? This was Cillian's way, and she was used to it, by now. It was a pity that Doll worshipped the ground his older brother walked on, for Nicky considered Cillian a manifest gobshite and an utter trial to be around. He possessed a certain kind of intelligence, a malicious restlessness that contracted to a sharp point whenever he discerned a vulnerability, and he liked to let his mouth run. When he did, as now, it was inevitable that something cruel and unwarranted would eventually come out of it. Everything to him was sourly amusing and fleeting, there to be derided and dispensed with.

'I'm going to get another drink,' Sara broke into the ensuing silence. 'Who wants one?'

'I reckon we all do,' Cillian said.

Sara shot him another wrathful look and headed out into the hall.

Nicky looked to Doll. A part of her did want him to say

something more to Cillian, futile as any further reprimand would be. But Doll only remained slumped in his seat, watching his brother in a sheepish trance. For a moment Nicky considered getting up and walking out, not just on Cillian but on Doll and the entire prospect of the night before her. Then she thought of the long drive home, the emptiness of the house waiting for her.

'Hennigan, do you remember Rubber Nallin?' Cillian said.

Nicky took a drink of her drink. She did remember Rubber Nallin. He had been a fixture in this house back when the drugs were still going.

'That's your mate whose nose fell off?' she said.

'Well now, it was only the septum that caved in on him,' Cillian said.

'What about Rubber Nallin?'

'Rubber's oul fella ran off while Rubber's mam was pregnant with him,' Cillian said. 'Whereas our oul fella, in fairness to him, he stuck it out for a good twenty years before deciding he'd had enough of us. I asked Rubber one time how he felt about his oul fella doing a runner before he even had a chance to meet him, and Rubber just shrugged and said he didn't feel any way about it. *You can't miss what you never had*, he reasoned. A wise man for a man with no septum. I put it to Rubber that he could at least console himself with the notion that if his oul fella had stuck around, he might have fallen so in love with Rubber it would never have crossed his mind to leave. Now, Rubber didn't agree, but the point is that's not a consolation available to myself or Doll.'

'The oul fella took a good long look at us, and he fucked off anyway,' Doll said.

'Hard not to take it personal,' Cillian said.

Sara came back with a fresh round of drinks. Cillian continued to hold court, reminiscing about the old wild times, about Rubber and the other varieties of lunatic that used to come around, the high jinks and set-tos that marked those vanished days. Nicky asked Doll once what had happened, and Doll said that according to Cillian he had decided to stop working with the crowd he'd been working with. Doll reckoned there must have been some sort of a falling-out, but Cillian would not admit to that and refused to say any more, which was fine so far as Nicky was concerned. Though it would be hypocritical to say she had not often enjoyed her visits here – along with Doll, she had partaken in whatever was going – she was glad that Cillian was apparently done with the dealing. Him she didn't give two shits about, but once he started letting Doll sell on his behalf – even if it seemed to be only occasionally, only in small batches, and generally only to certain of Doll's friends and classmates – that was enough to start making Nicky very nervous. Not just because of the illegality of it, the relative seriousness of the consequences if Doll ever got caught, but because of Cillian specifically. It wasn't just that he was a gobshite. It was that you couldn't trust him. He was reckless and complacent, and Nicky was sure that if things ever went wrong, he would have no compunction dragging anyone in his vicinity down with him.

*   *   *

They were still at Sara and Cillian's when the fireworks started up in town. They could hear the quick, staggered popping in the sky followed by faint flashes of light against the drawn curtains of the sitting-room window.

'You told your mother we were going to go watch that,' Nicky told Doll.

'I suppose we should so,' Doll said and stood up. 'We'd best be getting on to Cannon's, anyways,' he told Cillian.

Cillian picked the Ziploc bag of weed up off the coffee table and tossed it to Doll. 'Enjoy yourselves,' Cillian said.

Doll would not meet Nicky's eye as he tucked the bag away into his pocket.

4

It was a twenty-minute walk from Glen Gardens estate to Belleek Wood estate, where Keith Cannon lived. The fireworks continued overhead as Nicky and Doll made their way along the quays. The quays were near deserted. Most people who were out would be thronging the pubs up and around Main Street. Doll was quiet on the walk. Talk about his father tended to make him pensive and tetchy for a little while after.

Nicky walked silently alongside him and watched the fireworks burst and scatter in ragged burning streaks, watched the buildings and street lights on the far side of the Moy give way to the dark, bristling immensity of Belleek Wood. They crossed the third of the three bridges that spanned the river and shortly entered Belleek Wood estate. They made their way along a street of big, posh houses, landscaped front lawns, serious motors with new reges crowding the drives. Nicky cleared her throat. There was something nagging at her and she had to get it out.

'I thought Cillian was done with all that,' she said.

'With what?' Doll said.

'That bag he gave you. I thought he was done with all that.'

'He is,' Doll said.

'What are you doing with that bag, then?'

Doll looked at her and smiled thinly, like it was obvious.

'Cannon asked me to hook him up.'

'Cillian's not getting back into that, but you drop over to his and pick up a bag and bring it to a party?'

'All it is,' Doll said, 'is Cannon asked me last week if I could hook him up, so I said I'd check with Cillian if he'd anything going spare, and he did. That's it.'

'That's it?'

'Cillian's not back at anything. It's a once-off.'

'If Cannon asked you this time, he'll ask you again. You should have told him to fuck off.'

'What's the big deal?' Doll said.

'I just—' Nicky began, 'I wouldn't want you getting back into that.'

'I'm not getting back into nothing, Nicky,' Doll said, sharper now. 'Like I said, that's all done with. This is a once-off.'

'You don't tell me things,' Nicky said, 'so I have to ask.'

They got to Cannon's house. All the windows were lit up, the music and noise echoing inside discernible from the street. They walked up the drive in silence. The drive was filled with smooth, shiny black stones. The stones all seemed identically sized, like they had been made by a machine, and clicked neatly and solidly underfoot.

*   *   *

Inside, they headed for the kitchen, the noisiest part of the house. Keith Cannon was at the kitchen island with an older girl, a woman really. It took Nicky a second, but she knew her.

'If it isn't Hennigan and her bird, Doll,' Cannon said and slapped Doll on the back.

'All right, dickhead,' Doll said.

'Hello, Keith,' Nicky said.

Keith Cannon was captain of the school football team. He had a body almost like a grown man's – broad chest, muscly arms – but his face was a little boy's. He had delicate springs of curly hair like an overgrown cherub, too many freckles, a small pink mouth perpetually cocked into an expectant snarl.

'Delighted you could make it,' he said.

'Did you call that lad *Doll*?' the woman asked Cannon.

'Everyone calls him Doll,' Nicky said. 'Hello, Marina. It's Nicky. I used to work in Dillons with you.'

'I remember you, Nicky. Gosh, Dillons,' Marina said, and her long neck and cheeks flushed.

'Tell the lady why they call you Doll,' Cannon said, popping a can of Budweiser and giving it to Doll.

'My name's Donal,' Doll said, 'Only Doll's how I pronounced it when I was a little fella. I'd a speech thing for a while. And everyone in my family thought it was so funny, they never stopped calling me it.'

'That's sweet,' Marina said. 'And it suits you somehow.'

'You're right there, Marina,' Cannon chuckled, pressing the back of a hand caressingly to Doll's cheek. 'Look at that porcelain complexion.'

'Would you come away?' Doll said, ducking from Cannon's touch.

Dillons was the first pub Nicky ever worked in, her first job full stop. She'd been fourteen when she started. Marina had started at the same time and Nicky remembers that she was due to head off to college, to Trinity, which would have put her around eighteen. So she must have been twenty-one now, at least. She was tall and dressed differently to everyone else at the party. She was wearing a grey herringbone sports jacket, an incredibly thin, very pale green scarf wound in weightless coils around her neck, and toffee-coloured brogues dainty as a little boy's communion shoes.

Marina was different, and she'd been different back in Dillons, too. Right from the off, she had been argumentative with management, patronising with her workmates and downright contemptuous of customers. She loathed responsibility and was always looking for ways to justify cutting corners or dumping work on someone else's lap. She was one of those people who put twice as much effort and ingenuity into getting out of the work as the work itself would have entailed. Even though Nicky was the exact opposite of her – quietly and uncomplainingly getting on with things, completing whatever task she was assigned without issue – Marina recruited her as a friend, grabbing lunch with her and inviting her on her smoke breaks. Marina would take a seat on one of the kegs in the loading bay out back and give out yards to Nicky about any and every aspect of the job, what she saw as the consistent illogicality and rank favouritism in how the roster was scheduled, the political and cultural passivity and pig-ignorance of their workmates, the sadistic redundancy of so many of the duties they were required to perform, pausing only to bat away the flecks of ash collecting in the gutter of whichever enormous, half-disintegrated paperback – *Moby-Dick*, *Middlemarch*, books like that – was lying open on her knee. In retrospect it was obvious why she chose Nicky as her confidante: it was simply because Nicky was young and amenable, was the only person working in there who would tolerate Marina's rants. But Nicky had liked her; at the very least, Marina's inexhaustible capacity for complaint had been entertaining to behold, and helped pass the time, until she quit after barely a month.

'You were heading for Trinity last time I saw you,' Nicky said to her.

'I was. I did,' Marina said. 'Next year's my final year.'

'You're in Trinity?' Cannon said.

'I am,' Marina said.

'Knob End Central,' Cannon declared.

'Not unfair,' Marina said.

'What are you studying?' Nicky asked.

'English.'

Doll must have done something smart with his face – Nicky didn't catch it, but Doll's face could turn silkily insolent at the drop of a hat – because Marina looked at him and said, 'Draw whatever conclusions from that you wish.'

'I didn't say nothing,' Doll said.

'Don't mind him,' Cannon said. 'His surname's English, though he can hardly spell his own name.'

Marina frowned.

'English,' she said.

'Doll English,' Doll said.

'You're related to Cillian English?' Marina said.

'He's his brother,' Cannon said.

'Cillian English is a dickhead,' Marina said.

'I wouldn't dispute that,' Doll said.

'I was at a party once. Cillian English bit a guy on the ear.'

'Jesus Christ,' Cannon said.

'Hang on now, no,' Doll said, 'I know this story and that's completely wrong. Cillian bit no one on the ear. He did get in a fight with Hughie Cain, but Hughie was a big nu-metal head and he had all these piercings, including some big metal yoke through his ear. And yeah, they did get in an argument on account of Hughie owing him a few quid and a few swings did get thrown, but what happened was the edge of one of Cillian's knuckles got hooked on this thing in your man's ear, and like, he did tear the lobe a bit or whatever, but it was all an accident.'

'Were you there?' Marina said.

'Was I there?' Doll said. 'No, I wasn't there.'

'I was. I saw him step up to the guy from behind and just lunge in. Totally unprovoked, at least from what I saw.'

'Well,' Doll said. Nicky watched his bottom lip irresolutely twitch. 'That's what he told me happened.'

'Your brother, man,' Cannon guffawed. 'Speaking of, did you get that stuff for me?'

'Course I did.'

'Step into my office,' Cannon said, gesturing to the sliding door out on the back patio.

Nicky told Doll she'd grab a drink and follow him and Cannon out. Marina stayed with her, poured herself a large, fresh glass of red wine, offered Nicky one.

'So what has you at this party?' Nicky asked her.

'That's a good question,' Marina said. 'I was out for a walk last Monday evening when this obnoxiously loud car came flying down the lane. It pulled up next to me and there was Keith Cannon in a pair of wanker sunglasses behind the wheel. He said he was throwing a party at his place Friday night and I should drop in. On Monday that seemed like a profoundly sad prospect but as the week went on . . . no better option presented itself.' Marina raised her glass. 'So I decided getting drunk with a bunch of children on a Friday night just about beats getting drunk alone, or at home with my mother, God help me.'

Nicky wondered where Marina's friends were, the people her age she would have grown up with. Some were probably away working or travelling, but surely some had returned to Mayo for the summer, as Marina evidently had. Then an obvious possibility presented itself to Nicky, which was that Marina had no friends in Ballina.

Nicky took a sip of the wine.

Marina was watching her.

'Nicky *Hennigan*,' she said.

'That's me,' Nicky said.

'You're not in college yet?'

'Not yet. I'm going into the Leaving this year.'

'But you're going to go?'

'I'd no intention not to,' Nicky said.

'*No intention not to*,' Marina quoted, her brows rising. 'What do you think you'll study?'

'I don't know what I'd be good at,' Nicky said. 'Some business thing, maybe.'

'Something sensible?'

Nicky shrugged. 'You've got to do something.'

'And business is what you want to do?'

'If I get the points, sure. I want something I can get a job out of.'

'God, I can offer no advice there,' Marina said. 'And where would you like to go? Dublin?'

'I guess. I don't really know Dublin. I've only been a few times.'

'I didn't really know it either,' Marina said. 'Before I lived there, I only had a conception of it in my head.'

'And did it match that conception?'

'Certainly not. But then again, I can't really remember what that conception was. At some point it got absorbed into just being my life.'

'It's got to be better than here, right?'

Marina folded her arms.

'It's different. You're in a different place and in a different phase of your life. You're still in school, essentially, but in college you do get left to your own devices. Those big, draughty lecture halls. It's up to you if you're going to go to class and study and all that. You've lots of time to yourself. It can be hard to get used to. And you've to be careful to get living with a decent bunch of people.'

'The people you living with decent?'

'They are ... adequate,' Marina said, taking a gulp of her wine. 'So, is that Doll guy your boyfriend?'

'We're going out, yeah.'

'How long?'

'Couple of years, now.'

'That's a long time at your age,' Marina said, then, 'Sorry. That's a ridiculously condescending thing to say.'

'No bother,' Nicky said. 'You're just asking questions.'

'You don't want me to?'

'I'd tell you if I didn't.'

'Of course you would!' Marina said. 'Is he – will Doll head to college too, then?'

'You'd have to ask him.'

'Would he not follow you up to Dublin if you went there?'

'I wouldn't want to be the reason he goes to Dublin.'

Marina looked at her for a moment.

'No,' she said, 'you've got to want to do a thing for its own sake.' She took another drink of her wine. 'I didn't mean to come off like I was giving out to him or something, about his brother.'

'There's a lot of people who give out about Cillian English.'

'But there's his brother and there's him. It wouldn't be fair to, like, cast aspersions by association.'

'No,' Nicky said, 'it wouldn't be.'

'Anyway,' Marina said, 'I'm sorry for being judgemental, and I'm sorry for the twenty questions. I *hate* when people ask me what I'm going to do with *my* life, and here I am doing the same to you. And it's pointless, because the thing about the future is it's arriving either way.'

'So you're saying, what? Live in the now?'

'Oh God, I'm not advising anything,' Marina said, raising her glass as if to deflect her own statement.

'Do you've a boyfriend?' Nicky asked her.

For a moment Marina looked disarmed, then drew back behind a smile.

'I do not,' she said with a curious formality.

Her smile suggested she might elaborate. Nicky waited, but after a pause she nodded at Nicky's work shirt, the crest visible under her open hoodie.

'You work in the Pearl now?'

'I do.'

'I really couldn't handle Dillons.'

'I remember you reading your big books on your smoke break. *Moby-Dick* and all that,' Nicky said.

'My big books.' Marina smiled. 'I don't think I lasted a month, did I? I think you have to like being around people to do that kind of work, and I'm not a people person.'

'Neither am I.'

'No?'

'I just don't let them get to me.'

'That's wise,' Marina said, 'you're a wise woman, Nicky.'

She looked towards the sliding door Doll and Cannon had exited.

'Again, I'm trying not to cast aspersions, and I'm trying not to be presumptuous, but if I'm reading the situation correctly,' she said, 'your boyfriend brought drugs?'

'He did,' Nicky said.

'OK,' Marina said. 'Will we go have some?'

They found Doll and Cannon standing with a group of Cannon's mates a little way down the garden. A joint was being passed around. Marina took a hit, offered it to Nicky. Nicky took a hit. Doll was on the other side of the group, next to Cannon. The gloominess that had descended on him after leaving Cillian's seemed to have entirely lifted, his eyes bright now and a contented grin never leaving his face as, happily ingratiated, he listened to Cannon and the others trade stories and familiar jibes. Nicky intermittently ducked back into the kitchen. She had a second wine, and when the wine was gone, got back on the whiskey and Coke. After a while, Cannon and another lad, Michael Fox, started carrying pieces of patio furniture out into the garden and dropping them into the grass at intervals.

'What's happening now?' Marina asked Cannon.

'Obstacle course!' he crowed.

Joint hanging from his mouth and can in hand, he sprinted down the garden, cleared each chair but winged the table and brought it flashing after him onto the grass as he landed on his arse.

'Whatever, let's see ye do it!' Cannon exclaimed to a round of jeers as he jogged back up to the group.

Fox went next, then another couple of lads.

'This is so dumb,' Marina said.

'Go on now, Scully, on them long legs!' Cannon said.

Marina rolled her eyes and handed Nicky her wine glass. She slipped off her brogues and socks, left them on the patio wall next to Cannon and ran full pelt at the furniture, hurdling the lot with graceless abandon. The group cheered, impressed.

'Not bad now, Scully, but I have to disqualify you for abuse of a controlled substance,' Cannon said when Marina returned to the patio. Marina took her drink from Nicky and sat down on the patio wall.

Doll had taken the opportunity to walk around and come up behind Nicky. He slid his arms around her hips, knit his fingers at her navel. He nuzzled her ear.

'Here,' he murmured, 'come on inside.'

They grabbed another drink and wandered into the sitting room. A couple of lads were sat on the rug in front of the huge flat-screen TV. They had put on a video game, their heads bobbing and weaving along to the action on the screen. The game was a shooter, heads and body parts exploding loudly in frenetic, Saturday-morning cartoon colours. A crowd was gathered around, watching, some waiting a turn. Nicky and Doll found a spot on one of the couches and settled in. Doll began kissing Nicky. The kissing went on for several minutes. Nicky could feel all the concentration in his body flowing through his tongue and into her mouth, like a current. At times his kissing waned into an almost tender rhythm but then it would become emphatic again, his jaw muscles working concertedly away, like she was a glass of water he was trying to drink down. She supposed he was trying to be passionate, and trying to wear away, through physical attrition, the spikiness that had risen between them at several points in the night. Eventually Doll broke away and sat back and looked around the room with a satiated, softly startled look on his face, like he didn't know where he was and he didn't mind. The TV was bright, the room dark, full of the overlapping shadows of bodies.

Doll drew her in and kissed her gently on the temple.

'You all right?' he said.

'Sure,' she said.

She closed her eyes and felt waves pulse in the darkness of her head. She'd been drinking too quickly, was drunker than she thought.

'What you reckon's the story with that Scully one?' Doll said.

'What do you mean?' Nicky said.

'What's she doing here?'

'Here?'

'At this party.'

'She said Cannon invited her.'

'Cannon invited her, fair enough,' Doll said, 'but why did she come?'

'You'd have to ask her.'

Doll took a drink of his can.

'Cannon reckons she's going to fuck him,' he said.

'She thinks he's a knob.'

'He is a knob. Only she's kind of a knob too, in fairness.'

'I don't think she is.'

'Nobody asked her to have an opinion about my family.'

'You agreed with her!'

Doll's face clouded.

'Well, if she's not a knob, what is she so?'

'I think she's different to how she comes across.'

'Different how?'

'Just, in the way she acts. She's putting a lot of it on.'

'Well, I don't know how much of it's a put-on, but it'd be kind of fucked if she went off and rode Cannon. What age is she?'

'I really don't think she's going to ride Keith Cannon, whatever he thinks.'

'He says she's been following him around all night. *Giving me the eyes non-stop*, he says.'

'The eyes?'

'The eyes,' Doll said and raised his hand. 'Listen, it's all fine by me. Everyone can do what they want. Cannon certainly is up for it. I just think, whatever's going on with her, it's a bit odd she's at a party with young ones, you know?'

Nicky glared at Doll.

'What age is Sara Duane? She has like ten years on Cillian? What about that gap?'

'Yeah, but you know,' Doll stumbled, 'that's, like, a different situation.'

'It's not odd,' Nicky said, suddenly sick of the conversation, of what felt like Doll's wilful obtuseness. 'Cannon asked her here, so she came. It's not anything. It's normal. And who gives a shit what other people do?'

Doll drew back and Nicky could feel his leg go taut next to hers. He stared hard into the dark eye of his can, brought it to his mouth and paused.

'What's your problem?' he said. 'You've been edgy all night.'

'I've no problem,' Nicky said. 'I finish work, and even

though I'm wrecked tired I drive you around, I drive your mother around, I get to listen to your brother be a perfect cunt for three hours. I go where you want to go and do what you want to do. And that's all I do. Why would I have a problem?'

Doll smiled, as if astonished, and his smile faded.

'What the fuck,' he said. 'I thought we were having a good time.'

'Are you?'

'I am, yeah. I didn't know all this was such an ordeal for you.'

'You like things easy, Doll, that's what you like.'

'Do I?' he said softly, queryingly and then he emitted a single harsh laugh. 'Oh fuck me. Such a crime!'

'You never ask me what I want,' Nicky continued. Her voice sounded grating and dreadful in her own ears but even if what she was saying was wrong she knew she had to get it out. 'You just assume I want to do everything you want to do.'

'What the fuck,' Doll said.

He sprung up off the sofa. He began shaking his head.

'What are you doing here if you don't want to be here?' he sputtered.

Nicky did not know what else to say. She was burning with exposure. A couple of people had turned their attention from the TV. She glared levelly back at them until they looked away.

'It's fine, being here,' she managed.

'Then what the fuck are you talking about?' Doll demanded. His eyes were hard, his face flushed.

He kept standing there, waiting for her to say something else.

'I'm not actually making you do anything, Nicky,' he said finally. 'If all of this is such an ordeal, you can stop putting up with it any time you want.'

He struck the air in frustration and barged off through the crowd.

Nicky's face was hot. She touched her lips, raw and buzzing from the kissing. She took a drink of her drink. Her eyes drifted to the screen and she sat there watching, finishing her drink slow, letting the crunching gyrations and scudding flow of the game fill her mind.

The kitchen was acidly bright after the dim of the sitting room. Nicky poured another whiskey and Coke. She went to get ice from the freezer and a young fella was standing in front of the fridge with the freezer door open, his head in the freezer compartment.

'Hey,' Nicky said when he did not move.

The fella brought his head out. It was Teddy Cremin. He'd worked with Nicky in the Pearl last Christmas. His eyebrows were filigreed with crystals of ice. His cheeks were pink, capilleried.

'What are you doing, Teddy?' Nicky asked.

'Cooling off.'

'Is it that hot?'

'I feel, internally, very hot,' Teddy said, blinking rapidly and agitatedly, like he had something in his eyes. He was drunk, way drunker than Nicky.

'I think you need a drink of water,' Nicky told him.

'I was just thinking that,' Teddy said.

Nicky led Teddy to the kitchen island.

'How's your night going, Hennigan?' Teddy asked.

'Delightfully,' Nicky said. 'Wait there.'

She rinsed a glass, ran the water cold. Teddy stood beside her watching her perform these actions, breathing noisily through his nose with a drunk's brutish docility, ice vapour smoking coldly off his face.

'Drink,' she ordered, handing him the glass.

Teddy took a few mouthfuls.

'Keep going,' Nicky said.

'You're still in the Pearl?' he asked when he had finished the glass.

'I was in there today,' Nicky said.

'How's that creep Flynn?'

'Flynn is fine,' Nicky said. Kieron Flynn was her boss in the Pearl. The last thing she wanted to do now was talk about Flynn.

'Is he still in love with you?'

'Are you being funny?'

'He's does get awful goofy for the young ones, does Flynn,' Cremin said with a slurred chuckle.

'I don't know who Flynn gets goofy for, but it's not me,' Nicky said.

'You're not the first young one he's his eye on and you won't be the last, the paedophile. Poor old Doll English will have to watch out,' Cremin said. He went to take a step forward and staggered, grabbed the edge of the countertop to steady himself.

'Do you need to be run home, Teddy?' Nicky said. 'Only you're doddering on your axles a bit there.'

'Would you go away, Mammy,' he said, waving her off and pouring a neat whiskey for himself.

'Take it easy, fella,' Nicky said.

'I have a system,' Teddy said confidently. 'You have to have faith in the system.' He lifted the whiskey, toasted Nicky, and wandered off into the hall.

She downed a drink and then another, and went out into the back garden, expecting at any moment to bump into Doll. It took a lot to get him genuinely angry, but she had. She did not know what she would do when she saw him, whether she would double down and go at him again or plead with him to forgive her. Every feeling was coursing through her at once and she could not tell which one would prevail when the moment arrived. It might just come down to the look in his eye or the set of his mouth in that first second when she clocked him again.

But there was no sign of Doll. Cannon and Marina were still out there, Marina sitting on the patio wall, Cannon standing over her with his hands in his pockets, a joint smouldering in the crook of his smile. Marina had still not put her shoes back on. She was laughing wildly at something. Nicky could see her blue-stained teeth going all the way back into her mouth.

'Have you seen Doll?' she asked them.

'Last time I saw him he was with you,' Cannon said.

'Me and Nicky,' Marina said, 'we worked in Dillons together.'

'Yeah, Nicky said that already,' Cannon said.

'Nicky was sound to me. She was the only one with any kind of sense in there, even though she was only, like what? What age are you now, Nicky?' Marina's lids were fluttering, and there was a buzzing drag in her voice, the end of one word bumping up against the start of the next. The drink was wearing on everyone now. The party had reached that stage.

'I'm seventeen,' Nicky said.

'And that was ages back, sure you were only a child! What possessed your parents to let you out working in a pub that young?'

Nicky tried not to react, to pass over this remark with a glancing undemonstrative smile, but it was too late; Cannon cleared his throat and hung his head. Marina looked at him and then at Nicky.

'What?' she said.

'Nothing,' Nicky said, and then, 'My parents aren't alive. They weren't then, either.'

'What?' Marina barked. 'Why didn't you say?'

'It's a hard thing to say.'

'Oh God. I'm sorry, Nicky,' Marina said, 'I didn't know.'

'Why would you?'

'No one even told me,' Marina said self-pityingly.

'Don't worry about it.'

'Nicky's the hard-luck case who puts us all to shame,' Cannon said.

'That's me,' Nicky said, and she just walked away from them, down into the furthest, darkest part of the garden. Where the garden ended, beyond the glow of the domestic lights, the night turned dense between the trees. From what Nicky could see there was no wall or fence, no clear boundary to demarcate the end of the property. The level and ordered garden transitioned into a rising slope of brush and tangled briars and then into the boles of the trees that multiplied out into the vast depths of the woods. Belleek Wood itself was huge, extending out and around the town for a thousand acres.

She let slip a mindless slew of *fuck, fuck, fucks* under her breath, trying to draw the rancour out of herself like venom out of a wound. Poor Doll. He hadn't a clue, had he? But part of taking someone for granted was being sincerely ignorant of that very fact.

She was about to turn back when she heard something in the dark of the trees ahead of her. She listened, and heard it again: a series of stifled, rustling noises she figured was an animal, a neighbouring dog or cat or perhaps a fox, but then there came a fleeting snatch of a voice, as if from the darkness right in front of her. She held her breath and stood completely still. The voice had happened too suddenly and briefly for her to discern what it had said, if it had said anything at all. Her sense was only of a tone, which went sharply up, like at the end of a question or a reprimand or an order. The tone had seemed male. Behind her continued the ordinary din of the party. All it would take would be a few steps to be safely back within its radius. But something prevented her from moving, some sourceless tautness contained within the darkness in front of her. She watched the dark. It felt like the dark was watching back. Her eyes carefully combed the diagonal black slashes of the spaces between the trees for the merest trace of a figure or a movement. The thought repeating in her head was: *if I cannot see you, then you cannot see me.*

She stayed like that, for a half-minute, a minute, and then a laugh, ringing and clear, reached her from the floating clamour of the party and the spell of her paranoia was broken. All she saw was emptiness in the darkness between the trees.

She went back inside, fixed another drink. She talked to Ursula Davitt and Marnie Tull. She kept expecting to see Doll's head come wandering down the hall or for him to sidle up beside her out of nowhere. The party went on and then began to thin out. Without quite admitting to herself that that was what she was doing, she toured every room and corner of the house downstairs, then upstairs. She encountered a stuporous Teddy Cremin slumped on the stairs. She tapped him a couple of times on the jaw, asked him if he'd seen Doll, but he only rolled his head and muttered indecipherably. She'd tried once; this time she left the lad to his plight. If Doll was still here, she thought she would surely find him as people began to funnel out of the house, but he did not appear.

She went back out into the garden one final time. She looked around at the now empty patio, tins and empty bottles dotting every level plane and surface, the patio furniture strewn like wreckage in the grass. Cannon and Marina were gone. Whatever Marina was up to wasn't Nicky's problem. She'd get everything she deserved if she was daft enough to actually hook up with that young fella.

Finally, she took out her phone. She tried Doll's

number. It rang out. She tried again and this time left a voicemail.

'I don't know where you are but I'm about to head from Cannon's,' she said, trying to sound composed. 'The plan was to head to yours, so that's what I'm doing. I'll see you there.'

By the time Nicky found herself walking down Main Street it was after three in the morning, not another soul in sight, so late even the chippers were shut up. The debris from the opening night of the festival was everywhere; plastic cups skittered across the pavement, wrappers and styrofoam cartons and plastic cutlery jammed up the gutters. The unyielding yellow glare of the street lights deepened the shadows and made the shuttered shopfronts and abandoned streets look not just empty but skeletally exposed, like furniture with its upholstery ripped away.

A taxi crawled by, circled the tiny roundabout at the bottom of the street and came back up towards Nicky. The bars of the street lights slid like code along its shining black windscreen and then it was gone. Nicky hung a left at the roundabout and cut through the Dunnes car park, a centipede of shackled trolleys rattling lonesomely on their wheels in the breeze. Somewhere in the distance a dog started going off like a gun, a string of sudden, sharp barks echoing irregularly out across the night.

Nicky reached the Killala road and headed away from town, towards the stars and emptiness of the open countryside. Doll's place was a decent walk but she needed the air. She closed her eyes and the drunken waves were still coming, building from the back of her skull, cresting her scalp, and breaking right behind her eyes. At a certain point she'd just let go, stopped pacing herself and started chasing one drink with another, drinking whatever was right there in front of her. Now she was polluted.

Images, scenes from the night jostled in her mind. Doll's face flushing with indignation and real surprise as they argued. Marina's hapless, stammering embarrassment when Nicky told her about her parents; the way Marina looked at her, like Nicky had just slapped her in the face. *It's a hard thing to say.* That was true. The deeper memories flashed now, the ones that were always there, just below the surface of her thoughts. Her father and her mother. Tom and Eilis Hennigan. It was Eilis had got sick first, stomach cancer, and barely a year after that, Tom had received his lung cancer diagnosis. They did their treatments, the cancers went away for a while, then came back, then spread. Nicky was ten when the mother died, eleven when the father went.

'Brutal bad luck and nobody's fault,' she said out loud, quoting Cillian and picturing him hunched above his little rock garden, his slanted shoulders and devious needling mouth. Well, the prick was right about that.

She heard a car coming behind her, turned and looked down the road. She wiped her eyes with the sleeve of her hoodie. The street lights had ended at the town limits and the road was a swathe of darkness, thick as black cloth in the centre of which a pair of sharp white headlights burned towards her implacable as a fuse. She stepped deep into the ditch and watched as the car drew gradually closer and then all at once seemed to speed up and shoot right by her.

When the car was gone she stepped back out onto the road and resumed walking, sticking right along the edge of the macadam. She walked and walked until she was in sight of the English house.

In the drive she tried Doll again. His phone wasn't even ringing now. He must have switched it off and gone to bed. It hit her all over again that he'd simply left the party without saying a word to her, that even though it had taken her a while to cool off enough to do so, she had relented and did try to call him, she did leave him a message, and he had not only ignored her, he had left her to her own devices.

She became angry again and thought about knocking loudly until Doll, or more likely Sheila, came to the front door. But with this thought came a demoralising vision of breakfast tomorrow; Sheila scolding and deriding Doll for abandoning Nicky and obliging her to make her own way back here, and with this scolding would come the dogged petitioning of Nicky to agree that Doll was feckless and selfish and petulant, which he was, but which petitioning, the sheer overbearing incessancy of it, would, Nicky knew, begin to grate upon her until she reached a point where she could no longer endure it and then she would find herself defending Doll, arguing on his behalf against Sheila, which was the last thing she wanted to have to do tomorrow.

Instead, Nicky headed to the rear of the house, where Doll's bedroom was. As she came up along the dark density of the hedge she remembered the football, and a fresh wave of irritation went through her.

'For fuck's sake,' she said.

She groped about and found the soft, jawless skull of it in the hedge, pushed her arm deep into the scratchy, prickling lattice of privet and worked it free. She squeezed the dead ball between her palms like a melodeon, heard the final ghostly puff of more than a decade's worth of retained air escape it, and dumped it in the bin at the end of the drive.

At the back of the house, a wooden turf shed had been built directly beneath the window of Doll's bedroom. By the shed door there was a decrepit wicker chair with a concave dent worn into the seat from all the times Doll had stepped up and down onto it.

Nicky clambered onto the chair, reached up, gripped the corrugated brim of the galvanised roof's overhang, and using the chair and the brickwork of the house as footholds, scrambled and pulled until she had hauled herself up onto the top of the shed. She rolled onto her back and sat up. Stars and the sobering clarity of the air's gathering cold. Only then, already up on the shed's roof, did she think about whether Doll's bedroom window would be open or not, and if not, if she could make enough noise to rouse him from his drunken sleep. But the window was open, Doll's little metal ashtray perched on the sill, the stale, faded smell of weed discernible within.

She rapped the glass.

'Doll,' she hissed into the dark of the room.

She stuck her head in the window and listened for the sound of breathing. 'Doll,' she said again, at normal volume this time. Nothing.

She threw a leg over the sill, touched the floor, and climbed through. She groped her way over to the bed, waded her hand in the cool rumples of the unmade duvet. She turned on the bedside light and in the startling brightness the empty bed looked wrong. It looked like a mistake.

PART TWO

5

D EV WOKE up looking at the ceiling. His neck felt like someone had tried to axe it off in his sleep. When he slept, his head lurched around and settled at acute angles. The pill he took made him groggy but the sleep that followed was thin and turbulent, punctuated by obscure surgings of his pulse. He often woke, as now, exhausted, his heart drumming and cold coins of sweat pushing through his pores.

Dev hauled himself onto his elbow and swung his feet out onto the floor. His eyes stung like he'd been in water. He rubbed them and stretched his brittle neck side to side, the muscles gristling as he worked the sharp stiffness out. His T-shirt was damp, tacked to his shoulder blades. Already, he had a headache. He groped around, found his phone in the folds of his blanket. It was just after 6 a.m. He'd barely slept but he was wide awake. It felt like it had happened five minutes ago: the Ferdias showing up in the middle of the night, the kid, the kid trying to get away, the kid in the basement. Dev felt electrocuted with wakefulness.

He went downstairs. Gabe was out cold on the sofa, bare feet on the coffee table and head flung back, his TEQUILA PATROL jacket draped over his chest like a barber's bib. His socks were balled and wadded into his boots by the sofa, a vile waft coming up off his bloodlessly pale, gnarled feet.

Dev went on into the kitchen. The kitchen was how he'd left it, dented navy Corona bottlecaps littering the floor and the kid's runner tossed in a corner, the ceramic specks of the smashed plate starring the grouting and the bigger, bone-like chunks of it ranged along the skirting board, the kitchen chairs wrenched back and abandoned at stricken angles from the table. The morning sky through the long curtain-less window above the sink was as blue and clean as the ring of flame from a gas stove. It looked like the sky of another planet.

Dev walked around without touching anything, like he was still asleep. The quiet, the stillness, seemed imbued with the precarity of a dream. As a child he had suffered from deep and treacherously nested dreams, waking up from being pursued by something shapeless and coursing and awful, only to wake up again when the awful thing fol-lowed him out of the first dream and into what turned out not to be his life but a second dream framing the first.

Dev opened the back door and stepped outside. The grass was gleaming and crisp against his feet. He went as far as the low back wall and looked off out into the distance. What was always there was still there: field after field unevenly divided by dog-eared ditches and the grey curve of the narrow, single-lane road that disappeared and recurred amid the rises and drops of the landscape. The only house you could make out was the squat whitewashed bungalow that used to belong to Tom Mackle. It was more than a mile away, small and pale as an aspirin against the acres of green and brown. The mother used to drop in on Mackle on her evening walks. Mackle was half blind and he had got as far as his late seventies before he died. That was years back. Nobody had ever come to claim the place.

Dev heard a squawk and looked up. A crow was perched on the canted crossarm of an old utility pole in the field next to the garden. Back when Dev was a kid, a sequence of such poles had run across the fields with black power lines strung between them. On still days, when the wind dropped away, you could hear the insectile hum of the lines, low and insidious. They took down the lines, and most of the poles, well over a decade ago, and yet even now Dev sometimes found himself stood out here convinced he could hear the droning hum overhead, until he looked again and saw that there was nothing there but that single, stranded pole.

The crow flew down into the garden and began to pick its way across the grass. A crow's coat was black from a distance but if you got near enough and the light caught the plumage right you could see that the feathers were a deep navy folded through with tints of iridescence, like petrol in water. It was the way the feathers were layered, tight and overlapping as tiles of slate, that multiplied the navy into blackness. The crow hopped along and beaked at the grass with abrupt, darting movements that made Dev think of stop-motion animation or little machines. It got as far as the mother's old flower beds, overrun now with dock leaves and nettles, and lingered there to beak and twist with precise ferocity at something in the ground.

The mother had been digging out the flower beds on a mild midweek afternoon in early spring when the heart gave out on her. Dev was still working in Complere at the time, on the night shift, so he happened to be at home when it happened. As he usually did, he had slept into the early afternoon and was doing nothing, lazing about in his room, reading, half watching his little TV, until he got peckish and wandered downstairs to check with the mother what time the dinner was going on. He landed in the kitchen and could hear Georgie barking in the backyard, barking sharply and without interruption, and that struck him as odd only because the mother – who could silence that dog with the briefest look – would not tolerate Georgie barking away like that. When he stepped outside, it took him a moment to understand what he was looking at. Or not understand; the plain, absurd sight of his mother, lying flat on her back in the grass, Georgie barking excitedly by her head. As Dev walked towards her he laughed out of puzzled surprise, and called out *Mam* in a cautious and half-deriding tone, because all he could think was that this must be a cod, that his mother was pulling some sort of childish prank on him, and he did not want her to think that he had fallen for it, not for a moment.

*   *   *

The crow was squawking again. Dev touched his fore-head, pressed his fingers into the wall of bone behind the skin. The pain in his head was elusive and granular. He could feel it stir and sift and resettle in diffuse points with each push of his fingers. The pain vexed him, not because it was strong but because it seemed on the verge of dispersing, but would not.

'Stop,' he said out loud.

'Don't be,' he said.

'Don't be,' he said again in a sterner voice.

He was trying out voices. He wanted a voice that would be heeded.

'Who the fuck are you talking to?' a voice asked him.

Dev turned. Gabe was walking towards him, tapping a cigarette against a cigarette box.

'I'm talking to the birds,' Dev said.

'*Talking to the birds*,' Gabe quoted. When he reached Dev he lit his cigarette. He had smoker's hands; the tips of his fingers a deep, sour yellow, his nails rust-rimmed and the fat wart embossing the knuckle of his thumb tinted caramel brown. Gabe took a drag of the cigarette and immediately succumbed to a small coughing fit. He cleared his throat, re-cleared it, snorted emphatically and spat loudly into the grass. As he stood there in silence, regaining his composure, Dev could make out a recurring flecky hitch buried low in the rhythm of his breaths, like a playing card was snagged and fluttering in the spokes of his lungs.

'That's some morning,' Gabe said after a while. 'How'd you sleep?'

'I slept a bit,' Dev said. 'How about you?'

'Ropy enough on that bastard couch,' he admitted. 'You got anything decent in there for breakfast?'

'There's cereal. There's eggs.'

'Tell me you've coffee.'

'There's instant.'

'Nescafé?'

Dev nodded.

'Nescafé is tolerable. Sausages?'

'No sausages.'

'For fuck's sake,' Gabe said. 'There's three of us and that young fella to feed. We'll have to get a shop in at some stage, so.'

'If you'd let me know I could've got stuff in during the week.'

'Wasn't exactly a case we could just call ahead on this, Dev.'

'When are you going to talk to Cillian?'

'Don't you worry about English,' Gabe said, flicking the butt of his cigarette into the grass and stepping on it. 'Leave English to us.'

Gabe told Dev to make coffee while he went upstairs to wake Sketch. Gabe and Sketch came back into the kitchen, Sketch rubbing his face vigorously while he took in his surroundings, like he wasn't sure where he was. Denuded of its usual gloating composure, Sketch's face looked as pale and raw as a woman's without her make-up.

Sketch brought the kid up out of the basement. Doll looked shabbier and more defeated than the night before. The nick on his brow had opened and crusted over again.

He had arranged his ripped, half-buttonless shirt as neatly as he could. Sketch sat him down.

'Here,' Sketch said, snatching the runner from the floor and tossing it into the kid's lap, 'I can't be looking at you with the one shoe on.'

'You want coffee or tea?' Gabe said.

Doll did not answer.

'You sleep?' Gabe said.

'I don't know,' Doll said.

'You don't know if you slept?'

'I slept a bit, maybe.'

'Are you hanging?'

'A bit.'

'You look like you're hanging. How's the head?'

'I don't know.'

'You want a paracetamol? Dev, will you get this lad a paracetamol?'

'I don't want nothing,' Doll said.

'Don't be a martyr,' Gabe said. 'We'd this aunt. Sketch, remember Kitty? She was one of them ones who managed to always be a bit unwell, always suffering in some way, but she'd never take a painkiller. Which would have been her own business only she wasn't a bit stoic. She'd never stop going on about her aches and pains, how the head was at her and the stomach was at her and the back and the feet were at her. One time I said to her, I said, *Why don't you just take something if you're in so much pain, Kitty?* And she looked at me and she said, *Oh no, Gabriel, I couldn't do that*, and I said, *Why?* and she said, *Because then I'd be afraid I wouldn't be able to tell if the pain was getting worse.* Such a woman!'

From the cupboard above the cooker Dev brought down a Tupperware tub. The tub was crammed with the mother's old prescriptions, blister packs of pills, packets of plasters and green sachets of Lemsip. Dev tore two paracetamol from a pack and placed them down in front of the kid.

'Are you hungry?' Gabe asked Doll.

Doll said nothing.

'I can do him an egg,' Dev said.

'Do him an egg,' Gabe agreed. Addressing Doll again, he said, 'You want coffee or tea?'

Doll said nothing.

'We're just trying to be civil here, lad,' Gabe said.

'If he doesn't want to talk, we're as well stick him back down in the basement,' Sketch said.

Doll pushed his chair back, drew up his foot and rested his ankle on the knee of the opposing leg. He slid on the runner and started restringing the laces, worming them loose in their eyelets and tightening them back up.

'I'll have tea,' he said.

'That wasn't so hard, was it?' Gabe said.

Dev put a pan of water on the stove for the eggs. He fixed Doll a tea and brought it over. He could see marks on his wrists, a pair of angry pink rings bit into his skin.

'Don't go fucking it at anybody, now,' Sketch said.

'There'll be no more of that carry-on,' Gabe said.

'That was an awful childish stunt he pulled last night,' Sketch said.

'It was understandable to a degree,' Gabe said, watching Doll as he spoke. 'This isn't a usual situation. It's understandable the kid would be rattled. The unusualness of the situation, add in a bit of drink and it's understandable he might lose the head a little. But now things have calmed down, the kid can see there's no need for the dramatics.'

Gabe and Sketch had first showed up out of the blue at the afters to the mother's funeral. They told Dev they were awful sorry for his mam's death and that they'd been meaning to call out to him for ages. Dev didn't think much about that, the Ferdias lived in town and he'd never been close to them, and such sentiments were just something people said out of guilt in the moment, but a few months later, not long after Dev had quit his job in Complere, they showed up late one night, unannounced but with a rake of beer and a big pile of takeaway with them. This became a semi-regular thing, the Ferdias stopping by on random nights, watching movies and talking shite with Dev into the early hours. Then, one night, they told Dev they had something going they could maybe cut him in on if he was interested. Said it was good money, very good money, for doing next to nothing, and he wouldn't even have to leave the house to do that next to nothing. Dev had been out of work for a while by then, and though he was on the dole and still had a tidy sum from the payout on the mother's life insurance, that money was getting chipped away at bit by bit. So he said yeah, sure, and that's when the Ferdias told him that in that case he was going to have to meet a man named Mulrooney.

It was the early hours of a bitterly cold winter night when they showed up with Mulrooney, Dev shivering in the doorway as he watched them pull into the drive, half with the cold and half in dreadful anticipation, the tarmac speckled with frost, his breath spiralling smokily away from him into the night air.

The Ferdias got out accompanied by Mulrooney.

'So this is Dev Hendrick,' Mulrooney said.

'The man himself,' Gabe said.

Mulrooney looked to be a decent bit older than Gabe, likely his late forties. He had a woollen cap on, an open coat, a paunch under his jumper, curly tints of grey in the hair over his ears and mild brown eyes already fixed thoughtfully on Dev. Dev supposed that whatever a gangster should look like – scars, tattoos, a coarsened, daunting physique – Mulrooney was not it.

'What age are you, Dev?' he asked.

Dev told him his age. Mulrooney looked at the house, what he could see of it in the dark.

'And I believe your mother used to live here with you, only she passed the summer gone?'

'The spring gone.'

'The spring,' Mulrooney corrected himself with a quick condolent shake of the head. 'And you're here on your own, now?'

'I am.'

'Well, I don't want to keep you any more than I have to, Dev. Could we come in out of the cold for five minutes?'

Inside, Mulrooney accepted tea and nothing stronger. He sat with Dev in the sitting room and they talked. To an outside observer, their conversation might have seemed innocuous enough, turning on just those subjects of demography, property and logistics that animate nine-tenths of any rural exchange between strangers; who was living nearby, who owned what of the surrounding land, how busy the roads tended to be back this way. Dev did not feel as uneasy or intimidated as he imagined he was going to. The whole time Mulrooney was sat back in his chair, knit hands resting atop the sedate crest of his belly, talking in a voice that was measured and country-solicitous, assured and patient even at its most interrogative. It was the lively, frictionless register of a priest or minor politician working the room at a parish fundraiser.

Mulrooney wanted a tour. Dev showed the man around the house, the basement, then they went outside, down to the sheds at the end of the boreen. The ruts of the boreen had hardened like concrete, requiring them to watch their footing in the dark. By the time they got back inside the house, the lobes of Dev's ears and the tips of his fingers were throbbing viciously with the cold. Mulrooney swept off his hat, squirrelled it into his coat pocket and placed his hands on one of the sitting-room radiators. The rads were at their highest setting, so hot you would only be able to touch them for a second or two before the heat became intolerable, but Mulrooney kept his hands resting on them for five seconds, ten, long past what should have been bearable, composedly sucking air through his clenched teeth as the pain of the heat consumed the pain of the cold, before lifting his hands away and wringing them gently in the air.

'The lads here were telling me about your father,' he said.

'What about him?' Dev said.

'That he used to be in the Guards.'

'He used to be, a long time ago.'

'How long?'

'It's been, like, fifteen years since he finished with them.'

'Guards don't tend to leave that blessed vocation. Why did he?'

Dev shrugged.

'It didn't suit him,' he said.

'What didn't suit him about it?'

'I don't know. All of it, I suppose.'

'Dev's oul fella's a headcase,' Sketch piped up. 'Dev's mother stuck him in the mental.'

Mulrooney's brow lifted as he absorbed this information.

'And how is your father now?'

'He's still there.'

'Does he come around here much these days?'

'Not since the mother died.'

'Does anyone come out here?'

'Just them,' Dev said, nodding at Gabe and Sketch.

'It suits you, this remoteness?'

'It's just – it's just how it ended up.'

Mulrooney studied Dev's face, looked one more time around the room.

'OK,' he said eventually. 'The set-up you have here, Dev. It works, I think. When the lads first suggested using your house, they said it was because you were in a good location, but more than that, that you could be someone we could rely on, someone who could be very discreet, and now that I've met you, I believe they're right.'

'So we're good?' Gabe asked Mulrooney.

Mulrooney kept his eyes on Dev.

'I think we are,' he said. 'Are we, Dev?'

'We are,' Dev said.

'Only it does give me pause, this matter of your father. This connection, however old it is, leading back to the Guards, you know? I need your word that that's never going to become a thing.'

'It won't,' Dev said.

Mulrooney smiled.

'Even when it works out well, it never works out perfect, does it, Dev?'

'I suppose not,' Dev said.

At the door, when Dev, out of sheer relief at their impending departure, offered a rotely cordial 'We'll see you again', Mulrooney fixed him a look as he slid his hat back over his head.

'If things go as they should,' he said, 'it might be that you never will. Goodnight, now, Mr Hendrick.'

Dev brought the egg and toast over to the table, then tidied as the Ferdias talked to the kid. He gathered up the used bowls and cups and racked the dishes in the dishwasher, forcing himself to turn his back on the others for seconds at a time, his heart thrilling in anticipation and fear of the kid trying to make another run for it. But nothing happened. He got out the broom and pan and started sweeping up the pieces of shattered plate. Sketch, tailbone propped against the edge of the table, watched Dev with all his handsome conceit restored to his face.

'Your form's appalling,' he said.

'You do it, so,' Dev said.

'If I was doing it, I wouldn't be tracking right back over

where I just swept. Look at you, you're walking right back through it!'

'I'm just trying to get at . . . all the bits.'

'My mammy'd call this place a sty.'

'Sure, let her.'

'What do you think?' Sketch asked Doll.

'About what?' Doll said. He was craning his neck a little, looking out the kitchen window. From where he was sitting Dev knew he could see, at most, the back of the garden, the grades of the fields beyond, a featureless strip of sky, and nothing else.

'His form,' Sketch said. 'Did you ever see a man sweeping up like that?'

'Never mind about my form,' Dev said, brushing the pile of fragments into the pan and emptying the pan into the bin before renewing his sweeping with vigorous, patterned strokes.

'That's more like it!' Sketch said.

'I reckon this fella could do with the jacks and a wash,' Gabe said. 'Dev, do you've any gear you can throw his way? The state of that shirt, I can't be looking at it.'

'It's fine,' Doll said.

Gabe reached out, grabbed hold of the ragged top of the sleeve that had come away from the body of the shirt and tore the rest of the sleeve away from his arm.

'Like I said,' Gabe said, 'Dev will sort you.'

Most of Dev's wardrobe had been inherited, second- and often third-hand. Back in the day his mother and her friends would pass on to each other batches of clothing their respective children had outgrown. Dev was one of the youngest of the children in this network and was often the terminal recipient of many such batches. And though by his mid-teens he had outgrown even the tallest lads in his peer group to such an extent there seemed little point in his continued inclusion, still, his mother's friends insisted on sending her stuff until Dev turned eighteen. And the mother had kept everything. Every stray tracksuit bottom and jumper and T-shirt, every pair of boot-cut jeans and runners she had ever received on Dev's behalf were still here, packed away into his closet.

Dev picked out a T-shirt and tracksuit top. The tracksuit top was an old Mayo County football one in green and red. The T-shirt said NEVERMIND on it with an illustration of a yellow cartoon face with Xs for eyes and a tongue sticking out of the hapless squiggle of a mouth.

He stepped into the hall with the gear folded in a pile in his arms. He could hear the shower going. He knocked and Sketch opened the door a crack. Behind him, steam and heat, the clamour of the water hammering the bottom of the tub, the kid's body a smudged pink presence on the other side of the curtain.

'Good man, Dev,' Sketch said as he took the clothes, grinned and banged shut the door.

Downstairs, Gabe was gone. Dev checked the front. The drive was empty. He finished tidying in the kitchen and moved on to the sitting room, clearing the coffee table and fluffing the cushions.

Sketch and Doll came down, Doll in the gear Dev had picked out.

'Your brother's gone,' Dev said to Sketch.

'He'll do that,' Sketch said.

'Here, sit down,' he said to Doll, gesturing at the sofa. 'Throw something on the TV there, Dev, will you?'

'Like what?'

'A movie or something, whatever.'

There was an external drive with a library of hundreds of downloaded films plugged into the side of the TV. Dev scrolled through the library with the remote.

'What kind of thing you want to watch?' he asked.

Sketch frowned as he cracked his knuckles.

'Just, whatever, man, who gives a fuck.'

'I was watching *Wolf of Wall Street* the other night.'

'*Wolf of Wall Street*, so.'

Dev restarted the movie. Sketch sat down beside the kid on the sofa, produced the bag of weed they had confiscated from him. He rolled and lit a joint, offered it to the kid.

'I'm all right,' Doll said.

'Dev?' Sketch said.

Dev shook his head *No*.

'Sit down, man,' Sketch said, 'you're making me nervous.'

The only seat he could take was the wingback chair next to the fireplace. It was upholstered in red corduroy, the threading frayed and worn now, the seat nubbled thin and indelibly infused with the stink of dog. Dev did not tend to occupy this chair in the usual run of things, because he still thought of it as his father's chair, that appointed

spot to which his father retreated whenever his mood
began to turn low.

Back when Dev was only a kid, it seemed the father spent
vast amounts of his time mired in this chair, not just entire
days and evenings, but successive days and evenings, not
leaving the chair except to visit the bathroom, not going
anywhere, not going to work, barely eating, not talking to a
single soul, not even his wife and son, the chair dragged in
close to the fireplace like a door closed over against the
world. He had a way of sitting, one elbow resting on a chair
arm and the weight of his body resting on that elbow, his
shoulder and head cocked perilously forward, as if at any
moment he might yield and let himself keel over into the
flames, and he would somehow remain in that torturous
attitude for hours, gazing silently at the wavering, sparking
flames, or so it seemed in Dev's memory.

Once the father had arranged himself like that, installed
himself in the chair, at what had seemed an intolerable
proximity to the fire, it meant nobody could approach him
on any account, or even really be present in the room;
there Martin Hendrick would brood, or wallow in a mor-
bid silence indistinguishable from brooding, the heat of
the fire tightening against his skin until his mood – sunken,
black and completely undecryptable – finally reached some
inner point of culmination. Then he would get up and
leave the chair and begin to move about the house, active
again, but committed now to a quietly frenetic elusiveness.
He would devise innumerable methods of keeping himself
on the edge of things, out of the way of Dev and the mother.
He would disappear into the basement or a bedroom, off

down the back garden or out the boreen. He would assign himself tasks; inventorying his tools, tuning up his taxi, making minor repairs or putative improvements around the house and property. Often these tasks were unnecessary. He would, for instance, suddenly decide the light fixtures in the kitchen were not working properly, that there was a loose connection, though neither Dev nor the mother had noticed or thought so. He would clear everyone out of the kitchen and move a chair from one spot to another, climbing up onto it to tinker inscrutably with the guts of every socket in the ceiling, at the end of which procedure the lights would shine with the exact same brightness and fixity as before.

Then he might be gone for days, off out doing fourteen-, sixteen-hour taxi runs all over the county, working ten or twelve or eighteen days in a row, in relentless motion after each chairbound bout of incapacitation.

Always these cycles would begin with the wingback chair.

After the separation, Dev thought the mother might get rid of the chair, but she did not. Eventually he realised this wasn't out of sentiment. Getting rid of the chair would have been a definitive act, and to someone of his mother's worn-down and inveterately fateful cast of mind, definitive acts were acts of presumption, vulnerable to unforeseen consequences, and therefore reckless. The chair became a kind of protective charm and warning system: as long as it remained in its appointed spot, unoccupied, that meant the father was not here. And so the chair was left where it was, next to the fireplace, consigned to the purgatory of plain sight like something left rotting in an exhibit.

'Sit down,' Sketch repeated, this time with the firmness of a command.

Dev had no choice. He got down into the chair. He felt the hard edges of the seat springs press into his behind, felt the joints of the frame sink, lock and groan under his weight. For a moment, he thought the thing might splinter and collapse entirely beneath him, but it didn't.

Sketch smoked and watched the film with evident absorption. He offered Doll the joint, which Doll refused. He started up a running commentary on the film though neither Doll nor Dev encouraged him by contributing. Every time the woman in the film appeared onscreen, Sketch would groan and say things like 'Look at the unholy set on that beoir, what would you do to that one now?' He was trying, in his own brusque and unsubtle way, to settle the kid, to put him at some kind of ease.

Georgie came into the sitting room, scrambled up onto the sofa and whinged and nuzzled his head into Doll's ribs until Doll began to pet him. Soon a succession of happy burbles was escaping the corners of Georgie's black-lipped mouth. The whole routine was just like with the mother.

'What are you looking at?' Doll said abruptly to Dev.

Dev sat up.

'Nothing,' he said.

'You're looking at me.'

'How am I looking at you?'

'Just don't.'

Sketch broke his attention away from the screen to

glance in icy apprehension at Dev and then the kid. He grabbed Doll by the shoulder and jerked him forward with sufficient force such that Doll had to throw out his palms to stop himself from clattering into the coffee table, then jerked him back into place as Georgie's indignant barks filled the air.

'That fella can look at you any way he wants, all right?' Sketch said to Doll.

'All right,' Doll said, rubbing his shoulder.

'Here, go on,' Sketch said, suddenly companionable again, offering Doll the joint, 'you're as good as smoking it at this stage anyway.'

It was true that the smoke and the odour of it had filled the room. This time, Doll took the joint.

'I wasn't looking at anything,' Dev said. 'I was just thinking.'

'The big man was thinking,' Sketch said. 'What were you thinking about?'

'How in all its life that dog never had time for anyone but the mother. And now he's sat there cosying up to this fella.'

'Whatever your dog is at has nothing to do with me,' Doll said defensively.

Sketch took back the joint and considered Georgie's little head.

'It's a dog,' he said with distaste. 'I wouldn't put two seconds' thought into what's going through its mind.'

'That's all I was doing,' Dev said.

'I saw a thing on TV once,' Sketch continued, 'about how dogs experience the world. Their senses and all that.

You think there's the world, right, and in the world the sky is blue, grass is green, and shite smells bad. But for the dogs, it's not like that at all. What they hear, what they smell, the way they see light and colour, it's all fucked up and totally out of whack compared to us. The world is completely different to them.' Sketch took an unhappy drag of the joint. 'I don't like thinking about that.'

'The dog likes me,' Doll said, 'that's it.'

'What I'd like is a drink,' Sketch said. He looked at Doll. 'Here, go grab us some beers, will you?'

Doll looked at Sketch and then almost accusingly at Dev, like it was obvious Sketch had made a mistake and meant to address Dev.

'Go on, kid,' Sketch said. 'Get yourself one, too.'

Doll got up off the sofa. Georgie whined and resettled into the vacated spot. Dev watched the kid walk into the hall. Sketch never looked in Doll's direction. He just sat there, watching TV, the steady hint of a smile on his face. A moment later, over the noise of the film, Dev heard the faint suctioned pop and glassy chime of the fridge door open in the kitchen. Doll came back into the sitting room bearing three Coronas.

'Forgot an opener,' he said.

'Here,' Sketch said, gesturing at him to place the bottles on the coffee table. Sketch wrenched the cap off each bottle with his bare hands.

They drank the beers in silence. The TV kept up its reliable clamour. Georgie burbled into sleep.

Dev felt the balding thread of the armrest's corduroy against his palm. He became drowsy and found himself staring, heavy-lidded, into the black cavity of the fireplace.

The truth was that when the father finally went away to the Units the prevailing feeling had been one of relief. Neither Dev nor his mother ever quite admitted that to each other, but they did not have to. Peace had followed in his wake, an expanding and deepening peace that compounded day on day, and inside that peace they had arranged their little shared world. And even after the mother was gone, Dev had done his best, alone, to preserve the conditions of that arrangement. He knew, from the outside, how small and meagre it all might seem, but he had been living in a way that was his own. And then the Ferdias had arrived. They had insinuated themselves, bit by bit, into his life, and now they had brought the kid. It was an intrusion that had thrown things all off course. He could feel it in the pit of his stomach. Nothing now would be the same.

GABE ARRIVED back just after midday. Dev helped him bring in the shopping and beer from the car, while Sketch heated up two trays of frozen lasagne in the oven for lunch. The kid got through a couple of large servings, keeping his head down as he ate, as if abashed by the resilience of his appetite in the face of his circumstances. Dev could only manage a few bites of his portion before his stomach knotted up. Once they'd eaten, Gabe headed upstairs for a kip. Sketch and the kid returned to the sitting room to continue drinking and watching TV. Dev filled the dishwasher before going to join them, but as he came down the hall a cold, almost ecstatic, shiver bit and brushed down along the nape of his neck. He stood in place as a cloud of silver motes erupted in front of his eyes. He swallowed and his throat felt constricted and spongy, shrunken. He worked his jaws and his jaws began to tingle. He pressed his palms and forehead against the hallway wall to steady himself and closed his eyes, thinking he might throw up. He swallowed again, saliva oozing like paste down the shrinking keyhole of his throat. His heart was pounding and there was a racing ticking in his temples, like he'd just stopped sprinting. He pressed his palms firmly against the wall, concentrated on the solidity of the surface under his flesh. He closed his eyes and began breathing in through his nose and out through his mouth, in long, even draughts, counting as he breathed: three seconds in and five out. Three in, five out. In. Out. In. Out.

He counted and breathed and waited. He pictured the bare, grey surfaces of Dr Jarleth's room on the second floor of the GPs' offices in town, the stifling summer afternoons he spent there. Dr Jarleth telling Dev that *the body cannot stay in a permanently heightened state of alert.* Telling Dev to *think of your body as a machine. A machine has its processes. Even the bad things that happen to it are a process, and all processes end.*

Soon, the racing began to ease. The pounding in his chest faded. The attack was already on the way to being over. Then it was.

He decided what he would do. He went on into the sitting room.

Sketch was staring at the screen with a cold grin plastered on his face. Doll seemed to be paying attention too, or was managing a reasonable simulation of such, head up with his shoulders hunched forward.

'I'm going for a walk,' Dev said.

Sketch looked at him.

'You OK, fella?'

'Yeah,' Dev managed.

'A walk where?'

'Out the back. The boreen.'

'Any reason?'

'Just want air.'

'OK,' Sketch said, 'don't go anywhere too far.'

'I won't,' Dev said.

The boreen took him past the sheds, so dilapidated they looked prehistoric, their galvanised roofs rusted to the colour of dried blood, and then on past empty field after empty field, barbed-wire fences strung in rows along the edges of the fields. Around a mile from the house the boreen fed out into another field. Dev stood in the field and studied the sky. The clarity of the morning had burned away, leaving a grey, soiled gleam and a suggestion of waning heat, like a coin held too long in your hand. His headache was still there, muzzy and particulate, gritting up the corners of his thoughts; he reminded himself to take a paracetamol when he got back.

He started to cry a little, nothing much. All he wanted was to be alone. So far as Dev was concerned, the Ferdias could take that young fella away off to the end of the world, split his skull open and bury him in a ditch if it meant he could be alone again. Now that he was not alone, he was missing his mother.

By the time she died Moira Hendrick was so pervasive a presence in his life she had assumed a kind of invisibility, in that her effects were everywhere, so reliably dispersed Dev did not need to notice or acknowledge them, the way, when you grow up in a certain landscape, eventually you stop seeing it, because every last particle of it has been stamped upon your memory.

Mothers have powers, and Dev's mother had them all. She was relentless, clairvoyant, could bend her son's will so adeptly to hers it felt like it was happening the other way around. Her moods fed off and contaminated Dev's, and vice versa. She could bear in on him of course, could berate, hound and guilt-trip him like any mother, but she was the only living presence he could bear when he was at his lowest. Which was often. For as far back as he could remember, he had been prone to long, consuming lows, had only ever felt half alive, and half the time he wasn't even that. It was the mother that kept him going during the worst years. She had. Secondary school had almost been the end of him. Evenings he would stumble home hollowed out and hateful, the day's quota of humiliations looping compulsively in his head. He would slump down in front of the TV and put on *Home and Away*, a soap that followed the romantic agonies of a cast of beautiful teen-agers in a small Australian town. The town in *Home and Away* was a perpetually sun-drenched seaside idyll popu-lated by handsome blond surfers – golden shepherds with six packs – and devious but soft-hearted runaway girls with nose rings and rainbow streaks in their hair. *Home and Away* was the only thing that could make Dev forget about himself for half an hour. The mother would sense he was too raw for intervention, and without her seeming to enter or leave the room the tray of dinner would appear on the coffee table in front of him, then the custard and rhubarb, and then the tea and biscuits. Later in the night, as they watched the news and whatever movie that was on after the news, Dev's spirits would recover enough that they could become friendly, trading sarcastic commentary on what they were watching. She knew never to ask about his mood or how school was going.

Dev had been bullied badly in secondary school. At the time he could not name it. He could not bring himself to. But that's what it was. She knew, and knew not to say.

Dev was twelve when he started secondary school. He'd not properly hit puberty yet, but neither had many of the other lads in his class. The few that had, had not been transformed into broad-shouldered and bestubbled men, but had been subjected to a string of strange, uncomely manifestations – medieval sores and cracks erupting on their cheeks, rashy outbursts of hair, pains in their joints and a hoarse, hoopy crackling in their voices, as if adolescence was a permanent head cold.

Dev was still unremarkably sized then, on the smaller side even. And though he considered himself basically unattractive, small-eyed and with an unconvincing, doughy softness to his features, he did not think himself outstandingly physically odd; there were plenty of other lads who were dumpier or softer or goofier-looking than Dev, lads with squints and tics, with buck teeth, bad breath and sticky-out ears. In terms of his personality, Dev considered himself a nothing. He was mild and quiet, though not noticeably so. He did not think he came across weird or eccentric. He staked out only safe positions when he spoke and was vague and conformist in his publicly admitted views. He thought of himself as intrinsically unobjectionable, someone who, for better and for worse, could not be singled out in any way.

Then he turned thirteen and started growing, up and out, getting bigger and bigger. His voice grew deep. His limbs extended, and felt heavy, waterlogged. By second year he had become unignorable.

All boys, all children, are capable of cruelty at the right juncture of opportunity and circumstance, but only a few become committed prodigies of sadism; two years older than Dev but somehow in the same class, Joel Calmer was one of the rare boys for whom adolescence had been an enhancing process. By the time he was fifteen he looked eighteen. He was tall and strapping, with the streamlined silhouette of a swimmer and clear skin that looked tanned all year around. He was a good footballer, he was from a well-off, prominent local family, and he was effortlessly self-confident and popular, though much of this popularity, Dev can now see, was coerced, a product of Calmer's vicious extroversion and inherited social status.

One day Dev was stood by his locker, doing nothing at all, when he felt a sudden snatching weight descend on his backpack, and before he knew what had happened he was down, his legs gone out from under him and his tailbone aching from the whack it had received against the cold tile floor. The culprit, the student who had knocked him over, laughed once – a single joyless bellow, more like a shout – and carried on walking, not even bothering to look back to check his handiwork. Calmer.

Nothing happened for weeks after that, and Dev chalked that first incident down to happenstance, an arbitrary effusion of meanness the worst kids sometimes discharged indifferently to anyone in their vicinity. Then one lunchtime Dev found himself behind Calmer and his mates in the queue for the tuckshop. The tuckshop was a student-run business located in the basement of the original school building. A free-standing, solid wooden counter that served more as a barricade was arranged across the entrance to a small utility room out of which you could buy sweets, soft drinks and basic school supplies such as stencil sets and erasers. At least a couple of times a week, most typically during the rush before first class or at the mid-morning break, a restive clump of students would heave against and eventually topple the counter over and spill into the warren of the shop. While a few lads would actually try looting the tuckshop, for the majority the fun was simply in rushing and capsizing the counter, in the collective impulsive thrill of unserious destruction for its own sake.

Dev did not envy the lads detailed to run the tuckshop. Even on those days when the students did not turn into a mob, those working the till had to endure an incessant verbal barrage of taunts, threats and wheedling, complaints they were too slow and were mixing up orders, and endless accusations of short-changing.

This particular lunchtime it was Calmer up at the counter, berating the cashier, Johnny Clarke, because Calmer was short fifty cents for the bottle of Coke he wanted to buy.

'Just get a can, you've enough for a can,' Clarke said.

'I want a bottle, nancy boy,' Calmer said. 'I want something I can put a lid back on so it don't lose its fucking fizz.'

He turned from the counter and surveyed the boys behind him, his face a mask of granitic indignity. He looked past Dev, kept looking, then looked back at Dev.

'What's your name again?'

'Dev.'

'What?'

'Dev.'

'WHAT??' he shouted over the din of the other boys.

'DEV!'

'*Dev*,' Calmer quoted, his eyes igniting with intention. 'The fuck's Dev short for?'

'D-devereaux.'

'The fuck's a Devereaux?' Calmer snorted.

'It's my name.'

'Is there something wrong with you?' Calmer jeered, pointing a finger at Dev's temple.

'Nothing wrong with me,' Dev said.

Calmer ducked close and spoke low into Dev's ear.

'Here, Devereaux, have you a euro? Give me a euro.'

Dev's face went hot. His throat locked up, his hands clenched helplessly by his sides. Before he could respond, Calmer stepped right onto his toes, drew his head back and looked right into Dev's face. Dev can still recall the ghastly intimacy of that moment, the close gleam of Calmer's eyeballs and the sudden intrusive warmth of his breath as he thrust both his hands into Dev's pockets and groped around, fingers dabbling acquisitively around the thin inner fabric of Dev's trouser pockets, sliding over Dev's groin, Dev's prick, until he located and pulled out Dev's wallet.

Calmer took Dev's money, a single five-euro note, then went through the rest of the wallet. He held up and silently inspected each card – Dev's bus pass, the emergency debit card his man had given him, his Xtravision membership – and tossed the lot over his shoulder. When that was done, he tossed the wallet too.

'Cheers now, Devereaux,' Calmer announced, slapped Dev on the back like they were buddies, then turned to resume execrating Johnny Clarke behind the counter.

Dev still wonders now, from the long refuge of the present, why he was the one in the crowd Calmer singled out that day. Initially, he had put it down to his size, to the sheer obtrusiveness of his presence; Dev was the only lad in the year bigger than Calmer, and maybe Calmer didn't like that. Dev also wondered if there was not something he had said or done, unknowingly, at a prior moment in Calmer's presence, to which Calmer had taken offence. But what divined motive could possibly matter? In the end, Calmer did it because he could. From that day on, Calmer, and his little coterie of henchmen, knew Dev and watched out for him. Calmer's picking on Dev became habitual. In first year, Dev still had what you could loosely define as friends, lads who had gone to the same primary school as him and who did not mind his company, but as Calmer's bullying became regular in second and third year those boys began to be rapidly worn down by the social penalties incurred for associating with Dev. One by one, and then all at once, they turned on him for what they saw as his refusal to ever stand up for himself. It was especially vexing to them because Dev was bigger than Calmer, and so far as they were concerned, if he could have mustered sufficient bravery or recklessness or anger he surely could have taken some kind of stand against the older boy. But Dev could not help it. No matter how many times he was cornered by Calmer or his lieutenants, he never fought back, never once lost his temper and swung a punch, but neither did he ever disintegrate into the kind of weeping histrionics that might have persuaded the bullies that their campaign had run its course. What Dev did was take what they dished out; when they got up in his face he would go silent and impassive, submitting to each ordeal so that each ordeal could reach its conclusion as promptly as possible.

The problem was that this impassiveness enraged Calmer and his mates. There was a logic to bullying, which Dev, in his absolute capitulation, was thwarting; what bullies really got off on was stoking up and then emphatically extinguishing a victim's will, teasing a certain amount of resilience out of a victim the better to trample that resilience to pieces. The paradoxical thing about Dev's instinctual ragdoll submissiveness was that he could not be made more submissive no matter how viciously they tried, no matter how many times they spat on his head and punched him in the kidneys and booted him in the arse. Because he did not fight back, beating on Dev was easy, so easy it was pleasureless, and so pleasureless it became futile, which futility only provoked his frustrated tormentors into redoubling their efforts the next time around. So on the cycle went.

Once Dev's friends abandoned him, other boys began to avoid him. Victimhood was contagious. They did not want to catch it. By the end of his Junior cert year – the last state exam he ever took and scraped through by the skin of his teeth – Dev was almost entirely friendless, someone anyone could pick on.

Then, in fourth year, his final year in school, things got worse. That was the year after his father's worst break-down, when he took that German teacher out to the Silver Strand. Miss Lacey. He abducted the woman, basically, even if it was only for a couple of hours, but that was that. Into the Units he went and this incident, the rapidly circu-lating news of it, generated something worse than mockery or abuse. Now the other boys stopped reacting to him altogether. In the hallways, groups once indifferent to his presence now pointedly ceased their chatter when he drew close and only resumed talking once he was far enough away. Eventually, even his bullies abandoned him; Calmer and his mates moved on to other targets, lads with a bit of spark or spine to them, who could be baited into throwing back a punch. Dev became a ghost, unanimously unseen.

It was the loneliness of that year of school that nearly drove Dev mad. Moated by the collective disregard of the student body, his days became a quiet, empty hell of fric-tionless monotony with no one to speak to but the teachers that ever more seldomly called on him in class, because even the teachers seemed to have given up on him. His thoughts, unsolicited, unarticulated and stacking feverishly up inside his mind, began to feed on themselves, like penned rats. He had to keep his huge head constantly down, because he couldn't take those moments when another boy would accidently meet his eye and look ashamedly away. By the end he almost began to miss Calmer's beatings, because the beatings at least involved human contact. Calmer had seemed to hate Dev, but hate was at least an investment of sentiment, an acknowledgement. Now Dev had nothing and no one. He felt like he was becoming transparent, his skin and organs turning to glass. He felt like he was spinning through an endless void of outer space.

One night, at three in the morning, barefoot in his pyjamas, Dev stole out of the house and walked three miles to a field he had often noticed on the school bus into town. The field graded into a hill that ended in a steep, horseshoe-shaped cliff where a portion of the hill had been quarried out. As he made his way along the road in the pitch-black his eyes began to adjust and soon he could discern the differently shaded, deep blue contusions of the fields and the low, moonlight-flecked peaks of the mountains off in the distance. All the way along he was prepared to jump into the bushes by the side of the road if a car passed by, but none did. By the time he reached the field containing the quarried hill, his feet were sore and cut and wet and bleeding, and he further lacerated his feet as well as his hands and forearms clambering down into and over the dense, briar-knotted ditch.

Once he was up close he could see that the stony, dugout face of the hill did not afford as imposing a drop as he had imagined all those times he had glimpsed it from the window of the school bus. The drop was, at best, twenty feet, and did not look a convincingly fatal distance, but it was all he had. He picked his way up the shoulder of the hill, which was studded with small sharp stones and pebbles amid the larger static shapes of several sleeping sheep, pale and warm and seemingly indifferent to his presence. At the top of the hill, he inched to the edge and took a long look down. With a burst of black, demoralising relief in his chest he became convinced the drop was not sufficient. He could hurt himself, he thought, but he would not die.

He sat and waited, for what he did not know, until he began to get cold, lacing his arms around his drawn-up knees to preserve his body heat.

Eventually, behind him, he heard a dentate clicking coming up the hill. Hooves.

He turned and in the pall of the moonlight there appeared the candescent yellow eyes, long snout and raggedy beard of a goat, its ribbed, keratinous horns perceptible at first only as whorls of negative space in the dark. The goat stood off a few feet, its jaw meditatively chewing, and regarded Dev with concentrated intelligence. He looked at it. For a long time he looked at it, like it might speak, tell him what to do, but the goat just looked straight back at him. Finally, he turned away from the creature and set his mind to pretending it wasn't there. He sniffed and wiped at his wet eyes with the heels of his palms and stared hard into the black of the sky until he could make out again the radiant debris of the stars. He could feel the distinct stinging glow of the dozens of separate cuts and scrapes flecking his hands and feet. He examined his feet. The knuckles of his toes throbbed with the cold but the soles of his feet had progressed beyond pain, had turned numb and white as wax. For a moment, he imagined he was studying the feet of his own corpse. But he was still in his body. Where would he be if he was not? He was trying to imagine being dead, dead for all eternity. It was relatively easy to imagine death; death would just be a deep, oblivious sleep, a massive sedation you never come around from. Eternity was harder. Eternity defeated the compulsion to scale, to think in numbers and distance. Dev could imagine the passing of a hundred years, a thousand, and he was even able to hold in his head the idea, if only abstractly, of the passing of a million years, but the problem was that any span of time you could think of, no matter how enormously extended – a billion years, a trillion, a trillion-trillion – was nonetheless finite, a chunk of time that passed, and, by passing, ended. And if it ended, it wasn't eternity. And not only did eternity never end, it also followed that it must never begin, for a beginning was only another defined point, a division or boundary line, separating one chunk of time from another. So it had nothing to do with time at all. But where was it? How did you get to it? Or was it that it was already here, that you were already in it and always would be, and that, from the perspective of eternity, if eternity could be said to have a perspective, it made no difference if you were dead or alive, that in eternity you might be, simultaneously and forever, both? He did not like these ideas. He had thought over these ideas many times, and, each time, his mind could go only so far and no further.

Behind him the goat snorted. Dev turned back to it and watched it clotter to within touching distance. He put out his hand and the goat sniffed at it, quizzically, perhaps believing Dev was offering it something to eat. He opened his palm to show the goat *No* and the goat slipped its mouth around his forefinger and bit down. Dev screamed and wrenched his hand back. The goat reared a few steps and resumed observing Dev with its previous careful neutrality. Dev clutched his hand at the wrist. A band of throbbing white pain encircled his finger. It felt as if it had been bitten clean off, though Dev could see it was still there. He moaned and rocked in place and waited for the awful pain to subside. He was cold, sore all over, his finger was aching, and he was starving now too, he realised. Light began to crawl up off the horizon and he accepted that all he could do now was go back into his life. It was a pitiful little life, but it was his. Eyeballing the goat the whole way down, Dev descended the hill and got back out onto the road and began limping home.

About halfway back, he caught up with a farmer and a little girl in a school uniform driving a small herd of cattle along the road. Dev knew the farmer to see, but wasn't sure of his name. He surely looked a fright to the farmer and the girl, but, when they saw him, they did not appear put out by him. The farmer stalled the cows in the middle of the road.

'God almighty, the barefoot pilgrim,' he said in greeting, and then, 'You've been in the wars by the look of it.'

'I'm fine,' Dev said ridiculously.

'You're the Hendrick lad.'

Dev said he was.

'Young fella, you look as if you're in need of getting home, and I'm happy to run you back in the car, but I've these cows to direct to the parlour just down the road here first, and they can't wait. You're here now, so will you give us a hand?'

The cows milled benignly in the middle of the road. Their bodies radiated warmth. The pleasant smell of the dung caked into their haunches filled Dev's nostrils. He said he would. When they got to the entrance to the parlour, the farmer posted Dev at one end of the road and he and the girl funnelled the cows in through the gate.

As promised, the farmer drove Dev home. The mother looked like she'd seen a ghost when she opened the door on Dev and the farmer. After a wash, Dev finally told her everything; about Calmer, school, the feeling he had all the time now, like he was glass, like he was spinning in the endless void of outer space.

His mother listened to all this. She averted her face so he could not see her eyes. After he finished talking, she said, *Dev, if you can get a job, forget school.*

So Dev left school and got a job. He was sixteen. He was not dead. The job was initially part-time, in the Complere plant in Ballina, and when he turned eighteen, he went full-time. Complere made medical equipment. Dev worked on the line making ostomy bags. An ostomy bag was essentially a plastic, waterproof envelope with a seal cap that could be attached to a stoma. A stoma was any surgically made opening on the exterior of a body, allowing permanent access to the interior. The seal cap was placed over the stoma and the plastic envelope collected the internal wastes the body could not conventionally expel. The work was factory work, repetitive and relentless, but compared to school, Complere was paradise. Dev's co-workers were older, mostly in their thirties and forties, but despite the age gap they treated him the same as anyone else. There was banter and ribbing on the line; saying something daft or messing up provoked a mild flurry of heckles, but things never turned vindictive. Nobody picked on Dev, nobody singled him out. Dev enjoyed the company of the older people. They took things in their stride. They tackled each day, which was usually just like the day before, in a spirit of inured rue.

These were people who had settled into a way of life. They had their job, and most of them had a family of some kind, and beyond that the rest of the world was something to observe, to participate in and to speculate upon to a degree, but not a thing to become too invested in either way; on break the most popular subject, by far, was the job itself. The more experienced employees carped know-ledgeably over every small change to the schedule or production process, then complained all over again when the changes were walked back or further revised. They always knew better than management, took great satis-faction in forecasting the inevitable drawbacks to any proposed changes to procedure. They imagined they had a much more fractious relationship with management than they actually did. They gave out incessantly, but only to each other, and only on their own time. On the clock they always did what they were told and it wasn't like any of them were going to quit. It was a good job.

A year went by, then another. The grip that school had on Dev's imagination began to diminish. Once, when he was twenty or so and out in the pub with the rest of the

Complere crowd for that year's Christmas do, he saw the unmistakable brow of Joel Calmer coursing through the sea of heads in the lounge. Dev was not alone, he was with the others, but his body reacted; his guts began to churn and his heart sped up. Calmer seemed to be making his way in the direction of Dev, and he emerged from the crowd with the same lancing, interrogatory set to his face, coldly sizing up all around him. Calmer saw Dev and he stopped moving. For a full two seconds, three, he seemed to look right at Dev, then he just walked on by without any kind of change or shift in his expression.

Looking back on that moment, Dev wondered if Calmer, who by then was either in college or working himself, had not just ignored him, but had somehow not recognised him; as if all trace of Dev had slipped from Calmer's head. After all, Dev had managed what every other teenage boy only fantasised about: he had got out of school, he had quit the game for good. He wondered if this had not turned him into something unprocessable, a dead end or a hole scorched in the collective memory of his peers, someone whose fate had so completely and irrevocably deviated from everybody else's, it was like they had never existed at all.

Dev came through the gate into the garden. The back door was open. Gabe was sitting just inside it, the leg of his chair placed against the door to keep it ajar. He was in a vest and barefoot. There was a mug on the floor by his feet and he was smoking.

'Dev Hendrick,' he announced with a smile as Dev

came up to the door. 'I thought we'd another man making a run for it.'

'No fear of that,' Dev said, wiping his feet on the out-door mat. Then he sat down on the doorstep and began unlacing his boots.

'Such hatchbacks of *broga*, Dev,' Gabe said.

'You can't get my size in Ireland,' Dev said. 'I do have to order them in from Norway.'

'Jesus.'

'Did you sleep?'

'Like the dead.'

'How's all in there?'

'Them two seem to be getting on thick as thieves, now.'

'Sketch'd wear anyone down.'

'You should see him at the young ones,' Gabe said. 'He's not a man afraid of getting there by attrition. How would you say the kid was today?'

'How do you mean?' Dev said.

'Mood-wise. Has he been all right?'

'I guess so.'

'How's he been with you?'

Dev slid off a boot, looked up at Gabe.

'He was getting fierce insolent with you last night,' Gabe said. 'Even before he hit you the rap with the shoe and jumped you. I let it slide because of the circumstances. But I saw it.'

Dev shrugged like he didn't quite get what Gabe was saying, or it didn't matter.

'How long have they been in there drinking and smok-ing?' Gabe said.

'A while now. They're going slow. Or they were.'

'It's slow until it's not.'

Gabe ashed his cigarette into the mug by his foot.

'This situation,' he said, 'it's unusual. But it's nothing to be worried about.'

'I'm not worried.'

'Would you say that lad sitting in there now, drinking and smoking with Sketch – does it seem like he's here against his will, particularly?'

Dev pulled off his second boot, placed the boots next to his Crocs inside the door, lifted the Crocs out and began working them onto his feet.

'What do you want me to say?'

'I asked your opinion. I want your opinion.'

'The kid's sitting in there because he has to be sitting in there. He's smoking and drinking because Sketch wants him to.'

'I don't think he's suffering for it, all the same.'

'He did try and leave at one point. He tried to get out of the house, and you wouldn't let him.'

'You mean when he jumped you, Dev?'

'He jumped me, yeah, and he ran for it. He did want to leave, you'd have to say, and Sketch did have to stop him.'

'There's a context there, you know that.'

'I seen those marks on his wrists.'

Gabe looked at Dev. With deft, unseen nudges of his tongue he floated his cigarette from one corner of his mouth to the other.

'I would say that the kid is in decent nick, all told. We are keeping him fed and watered. You're just after going for a wander down the fields. I'm up from a sweet little kip. Before that we all had breakfast together, we had lunch. What we are trying to do is keep this situation civil, and I would say it's been a civil day, all told.'

Dev got up and made his way past Gabe.

'You're a great man for the civility,' he said.

'I am,' Gabe said.

'Can I ask you something?' Dev said as he brought the medicine box down out of the cabinet.

'Ask me anything you want.'

'It's about you.'

'Shoot.'

Dev ran a tap, palmed two paracetamol into his mouth, downed a big glug of water.

'You died,' he said.

'I did.'

'You died twice.'

'That's what they tell me.'

'That must be something to wrap your head around.'

'It is.'

'What was it like?'

'What was what like?'

'Being dead.'

'Well now,' Gabe drawled, 'that's the question, isn't it.'

'It is.'

Gabe took a drag of his cigarette.

'The thing is, the doctors said I was only clinically dead,' he said, 'they said it's more of a technical term than anything else.'

'It's got the word *dead* in it whatever it is,' Dev said.

An expression Dev could not read passed momentarily over Gabe's face. It seemed like he was about to say something, but he hesitated and then offered Dev a smile of tired malice.

'It felt like nothing,' he said.

'Nothing.'

'Nothing,' Gabe repeated. 'Lights out for good. Nothing.'

Dev remembered his mother by the flower beds, how, when he gathered enough courage to stand over her and look down at her, he had realised that a living body retains a tension, even when it is sleeping or otherwise unconscious, that is only evident once it is gone. What he remembered was the tensionlessness of her body, as if a cord had been cut.

'I just – I just thought there might have been more,' he said.

'The circles I run in, I meet more than my fair share of men who, let's just say, find themselves occupying an advanced state of parlousness. Men not long for this world one way or the other, who want to know what's coming down the tracks. They get a few drinks on them and sidle up to me and start asking me the same questions you are. And they don't like my answers any more than you. I reckon when it comes down to it, most men'd almost prefer hellfire and damnation over nothing at all.'

'Not me,' Dev said, 'I'd take nothing.'

'Would you now,' Gabe said. He tilted his head and screwed up his eyes as he blew a stem of smoke sideways.

'In any case I'll remind you what I reminded them. Which is that I'm no authority.'

'You're not?' Dev said.

'How could I be?' Gabe said. 'Amn't I still here with the rest of you?'

They had a dinner of sausage rolls, chicken wings in hot sauce and garlic bread, then Gabe got changed and announced he was heading out. Sketch put on *Enemy at the Gates*, then *10 Things I Hate About You*. When that movie ended, they caught the very tail end of the news, the weather report. The weatherman appeared to be standing in front of a map of Ireland with little digital cartoon suns and clouds and raindrops distributed across it, but Dev knew that in reality, the weatherman was standing in front of a green screen, a swathe of blank green fabric tacked to a wall of the studio, and that the pageant of sweeping gestures he was making were at nothing.

Sketch began to get tired. After a while he said it was time for the kid to go down for the night. Sketch took Doll down into the basement and Dev sat at the kitchen table. He heard no ructions or resistance. Sketch came back up and took the couch.

At some point Dev was woken up in his bed by headlights spooling and dipping across the ceiling and the sound of a car coming up the drive, a gathering hush or sigh, like the tide. His father used to come in at all hours.

He listened to the small, discreet noises of Gabe exiting the car, the faint crunch of his tread as he crossed the gravel. The front door opening and closing and, a minute later, the bassy murk of one Ferdia voice and then a second, drifting up from the sitting room. He tried to make out what they were saying, but their voices, at this remove, were too muffled to be decipherable. He fell asleep to the low fraternal rumblings of the Ferdia brothers.

7

Nicky woke up in Doll's bed, threw up in the toilet, and made her way downstairs. She had to pass through the sitting room to get to the kitchen. Everything in the Englishes' sitting room looked the same as it always did, the same only a little more shabby and palpable in the unlovely clarity of the sober, late-morning light: the sofa's greasy, toffee-coloured leatherette, so old sections of it appeared congealed, the pulverised cushions wadded like paper stuffing into the seat of the lamed rocking chair that no longer rocked, the old widescreen TV, its screen patinaed in a fuzz of glinting dust that made the back of Nicky's throat itch to look at. She came into the kitchen where Sheila, in her dark glasses, was looking out the window above the sink, waiting for the electric kettle as it rattled noisily to a boil in its cradle.

'There she is.' Sheila smiled. 'How's the head?'

'Not too bad,' Nicky lied.

'Sit down there now.'

Nicky sank gratefully into a seat at the kitchen table.

'Tea?'

'Sure.'

Sheila pulled back the dishwasher door and pulled two mugs from the jangling dentition of crockery crowding the upper rack.

'Would you be able for a bit of sausage and rasher?'

'No way,' Nicky winced.

Sheila fixed the teas and joined Nicky at the table. She asked about last night, where they went and who they saw. Nicky sipped sparely at her tea, hedging her answers, wary of letting slip anything that might suggest she and Doll had had a falling-out. As they spoke, Sheila glanced intermittently over Nicky's shoulder into the hallway, expecting at any moment that Doll would join them.

'He's not actually here,' Nicky said, with a little flutter of her conscience like she was finally admitting to a dishonesty.

'Oh?'

'We sort of lost each other at Cannon's party last night.'

'Doll's not here?'

'No.'

'Where is he if he's not here?'

'Cillian's, I'd say.'

'That would make sense,' Sheila said, sharpening her posture and removing her glasses to pinch the bridge of her nose. 'How is all at that man's place?' she asked.

'Quiet enough, actually,' Nicky said, paraphrasing Doll lest she inadvertently let slip her own opinion with regards to Cillian. She watched Sheila replace her glasses on her nose and wince as she rubbed gently the back of her neck.

'That migraine get you in the end?' Nicky said, recalling the exchange in the car yesterday and eager to change the subject.

'Oh now,' Sheila scoffed with subdued rue, 'it's not quite broken through, but it's certainly still hanging around and thinking about it.'

'Are you getting the, ah, the auras?'

Sheila looked at the kitchen window brimming with daylight.

'How bright does that sky look?' she asked Nicky.

'It looks a regular amount of bright,' Nicky said after a moment of consideration.

'That's what I thought,' Sheila said. 'So you came back here by yourself?'

'I did.'

'Did you get a taxi?'

'I walked it.'

'On your own? At what hour?'

'It was late,' Nicky admitted. 'But I liked the walk. My head needed it.'

'And that man just disappeared on you?'

'The party got fairly hectic,' Nicky said. 'I did try calling him, but I couldn't get him. I came here because we were supposed to come back here together.'

'He just took himself off to Cillian's.'

'Where else would he go?'

Sheila frowned as she worked through this information and its implications. She looked at Nicky.

'Any reason he might have gone off on you like that?'

'I don't know,' Nicky mumbled.

'I can't believe he would be that thoughtless,' Sheila tutted, permitting herself to turn scornful now that she believed she had a clear picture of events. 'Wandering off and leaving you to walk home alone in the middle of the night.'

'Like I said,' Nicky said, 'it all got a bit hectic.'

Nicky managed another few minutes of small talk before she had to excuse herself. She went back upstairs, dry-heaved over the bowl, and left the English house just before noon with a head on her like hammered shite and two Nurofen donated by Sheila dissolving in her belly. The Nurofen quelled the heaves enough to let the country air stir her hunger. She pitstopped at the Applegreen's and chanced a cinnamon bun she had to abandon to the ditch after a couple of bites.

As she entered Glen Gardens estate she did consider calling in to Cillian's to see Doll. But the idea of having to endure Cillian's presence for even two minutes while she was this hungover put her right off. Doll was likely still sleeping last night off, and Nicky was on a schedule today, she had work later. She collected her car and got straight out of there.

As she pulled out of the estate it began to rain. She came down along the quays, the promenade a blasted-grey wash, rain clustering and popping like bubble wrap on the windscreen, the Moy like lead. A gull was locked in mortal combat with a styrofoam carton, thrashing the flapping white box dementedly across the cobbled walkway. The cathedral car park was packed to overflowing, a hearse waiting by the front steps, light racing along the silver trim of its long, sleek body. The last time she had set foot in the cathedral had been for the father's funeral, and before that the mother's.

'Go on now, fuck off,' she said, and forced those memories out of her mind.

On Main Street the second day of the festival was tentatively under way. Several stalls were open but at this hour, and in this weather, there were only a few people about. Through the filter of her hangover everyone else looked hungover too, scurrying pale-faced and clench-shouldered through the rain.

Their place was out on the Foxford road. Nicky pulled into the car park, which was, as usual, three-quarters empty. The apartment building itself was not impressive. Its once cream exterior had faded to the stained, indistinct colour of a dead tooth, and the flower beds bordering the front green had been filled in with mounds of black plastic chips wrapped in sheets of polyurethane – a temporary-seeming, but now apparently indefinite, measure. Nicky parked, killed the engine and went upstairs.

The original family home was located on the outskirts of the village of Knockmore, six miles south of Ballina, on the shore of Lough Conn. After the parents died, it had gradually become too difficult a place for Nicky to be. Associations gestated and cracked out of every fixture and facet of the house; every light brown scratch in the banister's dark grain, the bottle of three-quarters-empty Fairy Liquid pushed to the back of the undersink press, the tallowy accumulations of grease pocking the grill of the cooker's range hood still so redolent of the Sunday fry-ups the father would cook ... the house was haunted, over-whelmed by their memory. And these associations, instead of fading with the passing of the years, seemed only to build in strength and number. Connor had understood when she told him she couldn't take living there any more. They sold the place last year and had been renting here since.

Inside, Nicky dropped her keys on the table and popped the fridge. She took a long draught of apple juice straight from the carton, checked her phone. Her shift started at four. It was already after one. She needed a wash and a sleep, in that order.

After her shower, she sat on the sofa in the sitting room and blow-dried her hair. The apartment walls were white and bare. Since moving in they had done little with the place. Connor had ceded the initiative of decorating entirely to her, but Nicky was not a person who needed to imprint herself domestically, to season a space with expressions of personality. The family photos from home were still under her bed, packed away in the box they had transported them in. Many of the appliances and furniture left behind by the previous tenants – the crappy kettle and undersized TV, the grim brown sitting-room curtains fashioned out of some sort of sticky synthetic – she had simply kept using. There were other, defunct items; a dead lava lamp pushed to the back of the modular shelf in the sitting toom, a stack of DVDs they had no way of watching, a hardback book of black-and-white photography and a cookbook, both so dis-piritingly generic-looking neither she nor Conner had ever bothered to leaf through either. But she had kept these things too. They were useless but benign, the kind of plausible clutter a life seemed to demand.

She went to bed and dreamt she was on a boat. A little row boat, red paint flaking from the curved planks of the hull, the prow nodding up and down. She saw dark, tufted masses of land in the distance, and knew where she was. She was on Lough Conn. The islands on Lough Conn were small and inhospitable, all rocky shorelines and meagre deposits of soil choked by thickets of knotted brush, though people had lived on several of the larger islands for centuries and continued to do so right up into the 1950s. Her father had told her all this. When she was a child he had taken her and Connor out to the islands, to walk among the still-standing ruins of the tiny stone cottages.

Her father was with her now. Tom Hennigan was sitting silently in the middle bench of the boat, wrists dangling in readiness from the handles of the oars trailing in the water. He was not paying attention to Nicky; beneath the tattered brim of his woollen grey flat cap his eyes were watching the water with calm consternation. Nicky followed his look. A dozen feet off their starboard side a formation of swimmers were gaining on them, their foreheads and shoulders flashing sleekly when they broke the surface, like seals.

'Those poor creatures are dying of the thirst,' her father announced in a tone of cold amusement.

Nicky knew what was happening. After the last of the people living on them left, the islands allegedly became a favoured haunt for bootleggers running illegal poteen distilleries. The legend goes that the bootleggers, before they in turn abandoned the islands, buried stockpiles of poteen across several of the islands. In the summers of his childhood, so her father had told her, local men in the know were reputed to swim out, dig up and take a single shot from each bottle, before reburying them and swimming to the next island. By the time they waded back into shore the men would be exhausted, merry, half-cut.

'We have to beat the fuckers to the draw,' her father said. He took up the oars and began rowing with grave determination. The boat jarred as they picked up speed, but instead of gliding forward the boat began to turn, to slew and then pitch. The lake seemed completely calm, but Nicky watched the bow rear suddenly up, at an angle so high she was sure they were about to go over. She bent low as she listed on the bench she was seated on, bracing her shoulders. A puddle of lake water sloshed in the bottom of the boat around her feet. She knew the lake was shocking cold. She was afraid.

'Daddy, be careful,' she heard herself plead.

'You could help instead of mewling like a babby,' her father said, his voice clear and bitter and urgent. Then the boat went over and she woke up.

Her alarm was beeping. Nicky reared up on her elbow and looked around the empty room. She wiped her eyes and plunged her head back onto the pillow. She did not like dreaming of her parents. Though in life she could only remember their kindness and patience and endless solicitude even as they became sicker and more fragile, in her dreams they were invariably restored to health, but in exchange were often angry or distant or furtive towards her, as if, preserved in the estranging medium of death, they no longer quite knew who she was.

When the alarm started going off again she realised she had fallen back asleep. She jumped out of bed. By the time she finished dressing and checked her phone again – still nothing from Doll – she saw that she was running late.

Nicky dashed off another text to Doll, *Call me when u get this. In work now. Hope yr nite was ok*, let herself in through an access door at the back of the Pearl and followed a corridor carpeted with thick red pile out into the hotel bar and restaurant. The far wall of the restaurant was a glowing bank of glass windows overlooking an outdoor terrace, the Moy and Belleek Wood on the far shore.

Rebecca Nicholson was manning the bar, which was already lively.

'Sorry, sorry, sorry,' Nicky said as soon as Rebecca clocked her. Nicky got straight into it taking orders. After a while Kieron Flynn came in through the archway and braked to a halt in front of her. Flynn was in his mid-thirties. He had broad shoulders and was a good foot taller than Nicky. He had a pierced brow and a skint head; the hair had started going on him a few years back, and he had finished the job before nature could take its course. He took a long, glowering look at her.

'For fuck's sake, Hennigan,' he said.

'I'm sorry,' she said, 'I got caught up . . .', but she hadn't the heart to finish the excuse.

'I can see by the head on you what you got caught up

in,' Flynn said, 'Look. This weekend, above all weekends, I need you here when you're supposed to be here.'

'I know,' Nicky said.

He pulled a bottle of Greenspot from the shelves and poured a shot. 'Drink that,' he ordered.

Nicky took the shot and downed it. She tried to say sorry again, but before she could even open her mouth Flynn waved a hand in dismissal.

'Go on,' he said, 'there's cattle need watering.' Then he turned on his heels and disappeared back through the archway.

'Look at the suffering lady,' Douglas Casey mused happily. He was sitting at his usual spot at the counter. He was a farmer. Most weekends he came in and ate his dinner up at the bar, a routine from which even the chaotic busyness of the festival had not deterred him. By his elbow the picked clean bones of a couple of lamb chops were crossed in a puddle of gravy on a plate, and next to the plate stood an empty glass, a glowing tidemark of milk coating the inside of it. Casey was perusing the laminated menu, his head cocked back and his reading glasses slid halfway down his long, seigneurial nose.

'I reckon you've everything on there memorised,' Nicky said to him.

'There's an enormous consolation,' Casey said, 'in knowing that you know your options. Can I ask is the jelly red jelly today?'

Nicky looked at Rebecca.

'It is indeed,' Rebecca said.

'Lovely. I will have the jelly and ice cream so.'

Rebecca took Casey's empty plate and glass and went off to the kitchen.

'At it hammer and tongs last night, were you?' Casey asked Nicky.

'It got away from me a bit, all right,' Nicky admitted.

'I bet it did,' Casey said with a chuckle.

As she worked away at the taps Nicky watched Flynn appear on the restaurant floor, complete a circuit of the room and head off into the kitchen. She was thinking about Cremin's comments from last night. Cremin was a little shit-stirrer, but his gloating little insinuations were not entirely without foundation. There had been this thing several months back; Flynn and Nicky had been going through a stocktake one afternoon, just the two of them, chatting away about nothing much, when Flynn, who she knew was into dirt bikes, asked if she wanted to come watch a rally he was racing in that night. He said it was a last-minute invite so no bother at all if she had plans or just wasn't interested, there was a bunch of other people going anyway, only he could get her in for free and there'd be drink tokens and the tokens would just go to waste if she couldn't come, but again, no worries either way. Nicky, more bemused than anything – she and Flynn got along fine she supposed, he was sound enough for a boss, but they were not friends in any real sense – said she'd see, though at that point she had no intention of going. But later, when she texted Doll to find out what he was at, it took him so long, hours, to get back to her and his response was so blasé – he said he was at Cillian's and he was going to hang there for the evening and she should come along if she wanted – that Nicky told him she couldn't actually, she was off to a work do instead.

The rally took place just outside the town of Castlebar in a large, torn-up field enclosed by a chain-link fence. When Nicky got there, a decent crowd – a lot of leather, a lot of facial hair – was milling in front of a row of shabby concession stands. Rock music blared muddily from tannoys over the snarl and putter of engines being tuned in the distance. Nicky found Flynn at one of the bar stands. She had assumed that when he said he was bringing *other people* he meant people from the Pearl, the likes of Rebecca and Cremin, but instead he was with three grown men Nicky did not recognise and whose names she forgot the instant he introduced them. Flynn, seemingly caught off guard by the fact that she had showed up at all, started yammering away with nervous animation about some technical racing stuff Nicky didn't understand or care about. She had never seen him like this before. At work he was terse, purposeful, practically dour. Now he was giddy, smiling mindlessly in his leather jumpsuit with logos stitched all across his back and down his arms, his tautly laced boots femininely narrow on his restless feet. After a few minutes he had to head off to the pits, leaving her stood there with his three random mates, Nicky nursing a flat lager in a plastic cup as rain began to spit out of a sky of bruised cloud. Eventually the riders came out on their bikes. The iridescent visors and elongated faceguards of their crash helmets made them look martial, alien. A starting pistol popped and the race began. Nicky gamely tried to pay attention as the swarm of bikes chainsawed around a course of furrowed gravel like bugs around a street light, but she lost track of Flynn's pla-cings and after, in the pub he insisted they all go to, she had to ask him where he finished. *Nowhere*, Flynn said, his mood of pre-race giddiness gone. *Sorry about that*, Nicky said. *It was good craic anyway*, Flynn said flatly. His mates stuck around for the one drink before promptly clearing out, leaving Nicky and Flynn alone in the back of the pub's near-deserted smoking area, the rain stuttering on the canvas awning above their heads. Nicky wanted to get out of there too, but Flynn twice came back with a fresh round of drinks before she could make her excuses.

She wasn't daft, by now it was obvious Flynn had engin-eered the situation. But if he had romantic designs, he remained grimly indirect in his pursuit of them. The con-versation, such as it was, proceeded in fits and starts, Flynn defaulting to work talk whenever things threatened to grind to a total halt, drawing repeatedly from a store of well-worn Pearl-centric stories and anecdotes Nicky had heard iterations of a million times before. Still, she laughed along when she was supposed to.

She watched him as he talked. Flynn's skint head made his facial features more pronounced, metal stud notched in the pale brown hairs of his eyebrow, his eyes bright above the stark blades of his cheekbones. Sometimes she thought he looked handsome in an austere way, at other times crone-like in his severity. More than once he told her that she was the only young one in there with any real sense, *you've a head on your shoulders* was how he put it, catching her eye for a moment then breaking away to look down the length of the smoking area with an apprehensive lick of his lips, like he was expecting someone to burst in on them at any moment.

Before he could steal away for a third round she told him she had to drive home and would be seeing double if she kept on the drink. When Flynn offered to give her a lift she told him that he'd as much drink on him as her. *Fair point*, he said. As he followed her out to the car park he performed flustered gestures of unsolicited gallantry, intercepting multiple doors for her and walking not alongside but just far enough behind her that she could not quite see him without turning her head. Her car was parked next to his, his motorcycle secured upright in the transport trailer behind it. Standing at her driver door, in the midst of saying a hurried goodbye, Nicky dropped her keys, cursed, and stooped to retrieve them in the dark. Seizing his chance, Flynn, in a low and pitiably earnest voice, said, 'Nicky.'

She stood back up but couldn't bring herself to look him in the eye.

'What?' she said.

'Nicky, there's something about you.'

The nape of her neck began to tingle and with as much feigned obliviousness as she could muster, she said, 'What about me?'

And Flynn tutted and said, 'C'mere,' and reached out and touched her arm, which obliged her to look into his face to see what he was going to do next and he did it, pressed his lips against hers, drily, and not even with much conviction. She pulled back.

'No, no, no,' she said.

'Why not?' he said.

'Well, I've a boyfriend for one.'

'That little scut,' Flynn said, and though she shouldn't have, Nicky did laugh, conceded a tame appeasing chuckle to that remark.

'That little scut is my boyfriend,' she said.

'Yeah,' Flynn said.

'And you're my boss, you know?'

'Yeah yeah yeah,' he chanted, as if in vehement agreement.

'So I wouldn't be thinking of you that way.'

'You're right,' he said, nodding and baring his teeth in a pained grin. 'You're right. I'm an eejit for thinking you'd be interested.'

'I'm sorry,' she said; she felt she had to say it.

'I'm the one who's sorry,' he said. 'I don't know what I was thinking.'

She watched him step back from her and shake his head and curse under his breath in a little fit of self-recrimination.

'It's just. I don't, uh, I don't want this to be weird for you, you know, down the line?' he said.

And she said it wouldn't be, assured him it wouldn't be, and since then she'd tried her best to just forget about the whole thing, which she pretty much had, until that little prick Cremin had started up with his provocation. She wondered if Cremin had actually got wind of her night with Flynn or if it was just a punt in the dark from him. Certainly, Nicky had told no one about it, not even Doll. But what had rattled her even more than people knowing her business was Cremin's claim that fancying young ones was a habit of Flynn's, which made her wonder if he had tried similar ruses with other girls; if what he had put her through was a play. At the time, stood there in the dark of the pub car park with him, his clumsiness, tentativeness and contrition had seemed sincere, and had inclined Nicky to write the whole thing off as a genuine mistake on his part, a misjudgement Flynn had not made before and would not make again. Now she wondered.

'Oh, my goodness,' Casey exclaimed as Rebecca returned bearing a bowl of jelly and ice cream. Rubbing his hands together he looked from Rebecca to Nicky with exaggerated relish. What he wanted now was to be lightly chastised by one or both women. Nicky decided to give him what he wanted.

'You're like a child on his birthday,' she told him.

'Oh, I am!' Casey crooned with delight. 'God help me, but I am!'

The evening went on. Nicky checked her phone a couple of times. Still nothing from Doll. Well, if that's how he wanted to play it, fair enough. Not long after seven a man came in and took a stool near Casey at the end of the counter. Even after a few minutes he had not appealed to Nicky or Rebecca for service. He just watched the door, his eyes following each newly arriving patron or group of patrons until they selected a table or booth and then his attention died away.

At a lull in service Nicky approached him and asked him if she could get him anything, because otherwise he was just taking up space at the bar.

'Bud,' he said.

A few feet away Casey was drinking a sherry – the only alcohol he ever touched – and talking away to Rebecca about how her schooling was going. Nicky brought the Budweiser over to the man.

'Now what's the story with you, Nicky, are you still in school?' Casey asked her.

'School?' Nicky said. 'Of course I am.'

'You must be nearly finished if you are.'

'Getting there, now.'

'And you'd be a Convent girl like Rebecca here?'

There were three secondary school institutions in Ballina. The Convent, for girls, Muredach's, the boys' college, and the Tech, a co-ed technical school.

'What makes you think I'm a Convent girl?' Nicky said.

'Because my mother always said that's where the good girls go, and you're the spit of a good girl.'

'You think so?' Nicky said.

'I reckon so. I reckon you're a Convent girl through and through.'

'Douglas here was telling me about his own school-days,' Rebecca said.

'Oh I was,' Casey said. 'I was saying how in winter you used have to bring a sod of turf with you, for the teacher. And the teacher would add that sod of turf to his little pileen next to the fireplace at the top of the room. And the teacher would be sat up there all day in front of that fire, feeding them sods in one by one, keeping his haunches nice and toasty, and the rest of the room like ice! Your fingers'd be so stiff with the cold you could hardly hold a pencil for to write out your name.'

'I hear they used to beat the heads off ye,' the man said.

'Beat you? Oh they would,' Casey said, half turning to acknowledge the man. 'In my day a teacher would beat the head off you without a second thought.'

'Absolutely leathering ye out of it, by all accounts,' the man continued. 'Clouts to the head, rapping you on the knuckles with brass rulers, kicking the legs of chairs right out from under you. Pure criminal battery, at least that's what my oul fella always said.'

'Well, your oul fella was right,' Casey said, clearing his throat as if he was not sure if he was being made fun of or not.

The man caught Nicky's eye and wagged the empty pint glass at her.

'Here. Another one of them.'

The man didn't say anything else after that, but that single interjection was enough to dampen Casey's spirits. After he finished his sherry the farmer bade his goodbyes and left.

The night grew busier. Even as the Pearl began to crowd up, the man stayed where he was. He had a scrawny neck, a long-boned face and reeked of cigarettes; every forty minutes or so he would slide a coaster over his pint, step off his stool and head out onto the terrace before returning reinfused with the stink of smoke. By then the bar was so busy that a couple of times he had to have a word with some young fella who, ostensibly heedless of the lidded pint, had commandeered the man's stool in his absence. Insisting on holding your spot like that was fine when the bar was quiet, Nicky thought, but with a crowd like they had in tonight you couldn't expect to keep your seat if you kept walking away from it. Nicky would have liked to say something to him, but she knew better. You got fellas like this in now and then. When he wasn't out smoking, he just sat in his self-appointed spot, broodingly scanning the crowd. Nicky knew what this man was waiting for, even if he didn't know it himself. He was waiting for the night's insult to present itself, and if it didn't, he might decide to invent it. It never took much to set a fella like this off. A stray look or ill-timed remark tossed into his vicinity. Anything and nothing.

It was when she brought him a fourth drink that he finally leaned in and said, 'What's your name?'

Nicky was already turning away from him as he spoke, so she pretended she didn't hear. Without meeting his eye, she made him his change, slapped it down on the counter and strode straight out through the archway and into the hall. The back lounge was out there and a row of little rooms they hired out for private functions. The door of one of the rooms was open, Flynn flipping stools onto tables. There was confetti and paper hats crushed into the carpet, empty wine bottles lolling in water-filled ice buckets.

'Here, I need a break from out front,' Nicky told him. 'Let me do this.'

Flynn seemed to catch the tightness in her tone.

'All right,' he said, and left her to it.

She picked up the bigger bits of litter, the paper hats, then ran the Hoover over the carpet. When she was done she wheeled the Hoover into a corner to cool down. The machine was so old and rickety you had to keep pumping the pedal over and over while feeding the cord in in short, taut sections. Any kinks or snarls and the spool would seize up. Nicky was whacking away at the pedal when she sensed a presence out in the hall. The man from the bar stepped into the room.

'I only want to know your name so I've something to call you,' he said.

'Never mind my name,' Nicky said, stepping clear of the cord heaped in a coil at her feet.

'How's Doll English keeping?' the man said.

'What?'

'He's your boyfriend, isn't he?'

Nicky looked at the man but didn't say anything.

'Only you haven't seen sight nor sound of him since last night, have you?' the man said.

Nicky's heart jumped in her chest. It hit her now, all at once, the blunt fact that she had not heard from Doll all day.

'Have any of you even copped on yet?' he continued.

'What are you talking about?'

The man put his palms out and smiled. 'Where is he?'

'I don't have time for this,' Nicky said.

She felt her face flush but the sharpness in her voice did nothing to the man's coldly smiling expression. Now she wanted to get out of the room. The door was open, it was only several short steps out into the hall, but he was blocking the doorway. She very much wanted to be out of the room.

'I want you to pass on a message,' the man said. 'You tell Cillian that we have Doll. He's staying with us and he's going to keep staying with us until Cillian gets us what he owes us. Tell the cunt he has until Monday night.'

'Is this a joke?' Nicky managed.

'No joke. Say what I said back to me.'

Nicky started walking right towards him. Her overriding impulse was to get past him and into the hall. For a moment he just stood there and watched her, but then he darted forward and dropped his foot on hers, pinning it. His head was close, angled. His eyes widened, a muscle jumped in his jaw and was still.

'There now,' he said.

He released her foot and Nicky stumbled backwards.

'Say what I said,' he said.

'You have Doll. Doll is staying with you,' Nicky said. 'And he's staying with you until Cillian gets what he owes you.'

'And when does he have to?'

'Monday night.'

'That's it,' the man said. 'Tell him I'm ringing tomorrow, and he better pick up.'

'Who are you?'

'Oh, he knows who I am,' the man said. He stepped into the hall and turned his back to her. On the back of his jacket, in gold lettering, was the phrase TEQUILA PATROL.

The plaster of the wall on her back was cool through the fabric of her shirt. There was a warm buzz coming off her left thigh, and Nicky suddenly realised that the man had hit her a dig when he was standing on her foot. Quick as a flash, but he had.

Though she knew it was pointless, she rang Doll. Nothing. She tried again and again, a feeling of crawling tightness working its way through her guts. The guilt she'd been feeling over their fight the night before revived now and combined with a fresh infusion of guilt for not having done more to get in touch with him today. It had suited her to take Doll's silence as an extended sulk on his part, a sulk she did not want to give in to. She should have known something was up. While Doll could lose the temper, his anger never lasted. He did not have the stamina for vindictiveness.

She was still against the wall trying Doll when Flynn came in.

'You're taking your time,' he said.

She pulled the phone away from her ear.

'You all right?' Flynn said. He looked concerned, and his assumption that he could offer her his concern made Nicky angrier.

'Oh, fuck off,' she said.

'What did I do?' he said, but his cheeks coloured as he spoke.

'I think I might have to go,' Nicky said.

'What happened?' Flynn said. 'Nicky?'

'Nothing,' she said. 'Just a guy – your usual creep, demands a chat even though you tell him you don't want to. I told him to fuck off.'

'That was it?' Flynn said. She could tell he knew she was not telling him everything.

'I just might have to knock off early,' she said. 'I'm sorry.'

'OK,' Flynn said, 'but come out front with me first. If that fella is still here, I want you to point him out to me.'

'It's all right,' Nicky said. Already she regretted saying anything. The last thing she wanted was to give Flynn an excuse to be at all chivalrous towards her.

'Nicky,' he said.

'OK, OK,' she said.

They went out front. The seat was empty. No coaster on the pint.

8

Sunday morning, Dev slept until almost nine. He came downstairs to crumbed plates and mugs cradling the pale dregs of cold tea, sausages, rashers and eggs congealing waxily in a pan on the cooker top.

Through the kitchen window he could see the Ferdias at the bottom of the garden. The back door was closed. Dev felt that this was deliberate, a sign that they required privacy, the privacy of everything beyond the house. As in a dream where you are compelled, helplessly, to do the exact opposite of what you know you should do, he opened the door and went out to them. Gabe had his back to him, mobile phone to his ear, shoulders tautly squared. Dev could hear him saying *yeah*, *yeah*, *yeah* into the phone in an urgent and placating way.

Sketch clocked Dev and intercepted him before he could get too close.

'There he is,' he said. 'Sleeping Beauty.'

'What's happening?' Dev said.

Sketch glanced at his brother, then back at Dev.

'He's on to Mulrooney,' he said, walking away from Gabe with a collusive cock of the head that bid Dev follow him. 'Just giving him an update, keeping him in the loop.'

'You talked to Cillian yet?' Dev said.

'Never mind about Cillian,' Sketch said. 'Word was delivered to that buck last night. He's in the loop, too.'

'When's this going to be over?'

Dev followed Sketch's eyes, which went to his brother. Gabe turned and saw them watching him. He was so absorbed in the call that his eyes seemed to slide over Dev with a cold glaze of unrecognition, as if Dev were a stranger on the street with whom he had happened to make eye contact. Then Gabe blinked, and it was as if he suddenly realised Dev was Dev. He smiled unhappily and turned away again.

'Imminently, fella. The machine is in motion. Here,' Sketch said. He pulled a pair of snips out of his jeans pocket. 'What you can do is get the kid up and fed and give us five minutes more here.'

In the kitchen, Dev lifted the keys from the hook. He stood in front of the basement door and stilled himself and listened; he imagined Doll braced and breathing through his nose on just the other side, ready to rush him as soon as he opened the door.

He put the key in the lock and said, 'I am opening the door.'

The basement was blindingly dark. He snapped on the light. He saw the shape of Doll on the bed flinch as the space erupted into brightness.

He came down the steps. Doll was lying on his side on

the mattress, his hands out of sight like he was trying to hide something. He lifted his head over his shoulder to see who was coming.

Dev came around the side of the bed frame. Doll's wrists were tied to the bedpost. It looked like he could lie on his side, or sit up somewhat, but he could not get off the mattress.

'Steady on, now,' Dev said, working the jaws of the snips in between the kid's wrists. Doll sighed and hissed with distress. Dev snapped the zip tie. Doll rolled onto his back and groaned. He turned his arms in slow circles in the air and flexed his fingers.

'Christ,' he said.

The bedsheet was puddled on the floor by the bed.

'Weren't you cold down here?' Dev said.

'My hands are killing me,' Doll said.

He sat up and swung his legs over the side, arms hanging limply between his legs. He looked dismal. Tears clung to his lashes. He was looking at his hands. Dev did not know what to say. He had noticed the kid's wrists yesterday. He knew they must have been tying him up at night. It was still a shock to see.

Georgie appeared at the top of the steps, trotted down to them and discharged a couple of inquisitive barks.

'I should put him in here with you,' Dev said, relieved there was something else he could put his attention on.

'Don't do that,' Doll said, touching his face.

'I'm kidding.'

'You put that dog in with me and I will . . . murder the thing. I'll make it suffer.'

'There's no call for that,' Dev said.

'Don't say another word to me about that fucking dog. You and that dog.'

'That's my mother's dog, you stupid little shit,' Dev said. 'I don't give a fuck about you. No one gives a fuck about you, and that's the truth. Why are you even here? No one gives a shit. That's why.'

Dev's face was hot, blood beating in his cheeks.

'I didn't do anything,' Doll said miserably.

Dev picked the sheet up off the floor, went to gather in its folds, then threw it down again.

'You bring that up. The pillow, too,' he said.

Even as he issued this order, a part of him was convinced that Doll would not comply, but he did. Dev watched as the kid came off the bed, bent over and dutifully gathered up the sheet, then the pillow.

'Go on,' Dev said, waiting as Doll plodded ahead of him up the stairs.

Dev heated back up the fry, fixed a plate for the kid. He rested his tailbone against the counter, facing the kid, drinking a cup of tea. When he shifted a few degrees he could see out into the back garden. Gabe and Sketch were still there, huddled together by the rear wall, deep in conversation.

As Doll ate, Georgie danced around the legs of his chair. With a flick of his knife, Doll sent a gobbet of rasher to the floor. Georgie snatched the gobbet up before it even hit the ground.

'Sorry for saying that,' Doll said.

Dev looked at him, supped his tea.

'I wouldn't touch that dog. I wouldn't do nothing to a defenceless creature,' Doll said.

'You were upset.'

'I wasn't upset,' Doll said. He frowned. 'It's just – it's a joke.'

'It's not a usual situation,' Dev said.

'They out there?'

'They are.'

'What are they talking about?'

'I don't know.'

'You don't know?'

'No.'

'You should, man. You help a couple of lads kidnap someone you should know what they're talking about.' Doll looked straight at Dev as he said this. His face coloured. His mouth went tight. Then he went back to his food.

'You know something,' he said after a while.

'What?' Dev said.

'I ran into a fella in town on Friday, and his name was Hendrick.'

'Yeah?'

'Yeah. Tall fella, almost as tall as you. At the district hospital. Right by the Units. Sat there on the steps having a smoke like he'd all the time in the world. By his age he could be your oul fella.'

Dev's heart swooped in his chest. He blinked, cleared his throat.

'I'd nearly say he was,' Dev said, caught too off guard to dissemble.

'He asked me to put a bet on for him.'

'He likes the horses.'

'Dogs, actually.'

'Likes the dogs, too.'

'The dog was called—' Doll placed the knife down on the edge of his plate. He took a gulp of his tea. 'It was called . . . I wonder if it came in?'

'It's not often they come in for him.'

'Perilous Endeavour,' Doll said. 'Eight to one. I put twenty-five quid on for him. He asked me to put twenty on and take five commission for myself, but once I was in the shop I thought fuck it and put the whole lot on for him.'

'Sound of you,' Dev said.

'Yeah, sound,' Doll said. He dropped a hand, cradled Georgie's head for a second.

Dev put his cup down on the counter. The ends of his fingers felt cold, trembly.

'He knew me, knew the head of me. Said he knew my oul fella. Used to run him around in the taxis and all that.'

'He ran a lot of fellas around in taxis.'

'I know, but still, it's fucked how quick it all twists together,' Doll said, 'when you go back a bit.'

'It is,' Dev said.

'Twenty-five times eight,' Doll said. 'Times four's a hundred. That's two hundred quid he could have won.'

'That'll make his weekend, so,' Dev said. The father had a habit of roping other people into placing bets for him, because he didn't like going into town himself. He'd roped Dev into putting a few on for him in the past.

'He said he lives in the Units,' Doll said, flicking another scrap to the ground. 'Why's he live there?'

'Why would anyone live there?' Dev said.

Doll looked around the kitchen, then back at Dev.

'Your mother did die, didn't she?'

'She did,' Dev said.

Doll watched the dog eating by his foot, the repeating eager bob of its head.

'I'm not scared of you, you know,' he said.

Dev brought Doll more tea, then gathered the bedding from where the kid had dropped it on a chair and carried it over to the washing machine. He popped open the washing-machine door and began feeding the bedclothes into the cool metal cavity of the drum. He had his back to Doll as he did this.

'Is it true what Sketch said?' Doll said.

'What did he say?'

'He said we're out in the middle of nowhere. Is that true?'

'It's a remote enough spot.'

'I bet it's not too far,' Doll said. 'You went to school in Ballina. It can't be that far.'

'I could've moved since.'

'I reckon you been here a long time.'

Dev said nothing to this. He came over to the sink, retrieved the bottle of detergent from the cupboard. Doll was watching his every move.

'The same day they grab me I run into your oul fella,' Doll said. 'What's that mean?'

Dev looked at him.

'It's got to mean something,' Doll said.

'Everything means something,' Dev said.

'My girlfriend figured out who he was. Martin Hendrick. The taxi driver who kidnapped that teacher. Your oul fella a kidnapper too. What are the odds?'

'That man wasn't well. He wasn't well then, and he isn't now.'

'Are you?'

'Am I what?'

'Are you well?'

Dev returned to the washing machine and with shaking hands poured a measure of the floral-smelling liquid into the cup. He bent down and placed the cup on the mound of clothes at the very back of the drum as carefully as if it contained a naked flame. The inside of the drum was dark and gleaming, divided by metal ridges, the curved panels between the ridges studded with holes. It always reminded Dev of outer space, of the squeezed, claustrophobic compartment of a spaceship or a space helmet.

'I could leave now, you know,' Doll said. 'I could shoot straight out that front door. Give me two minutes' head start and I'm good, man.'

Dev's heart swooped again. He closed his eyes, opened them.

'You seemed grand enough here, yesterday,' he said, resorting to Gabe's argument, 'sat in there drinking beers and watching films with the other lad.'

He was stooped, bent close enough to the door of the

washing machine that, as he spoke, his voice resonated metallically in the drum.

'Say you turned around and I was gone,' Doll explained. 'Say I jumped you. Say what you like. What can they do? This is your house.'

'They want you here,' Dev said. He knew he should turn around and keep eyes on the kid. Yet he felt so long as he abstained from this impulse to look, so long as the kid remained merely a voice over his shoulder, nothing would happen.

'You know I don't want to be here. You know you don't want me here either, man.'

'It's not my decision,' Dev said.

'How's it not your decision?'

Dev swung shut the washing machine's door. He stood up, pressed the start button. There was an internal locking noise, a deep preliminary gurgle, and then the entire enormous appliance shuddered and hummed into activity. Dev turned to face the kid.

'Why would you want any of this shit in your house?' Doll said. He was sitting forward, the heels of his palms pressed against his knees like he was holding himself in place. 'Who cares if I go? They know where my mother's house is. They can come around any time they want. What's the point of any of this? It's a joke.'

'Tell that to them,' Dev said.

'Just give me a phone, man,' Doll said. 'Just let me call the mother so she knows I'm OK. Just that, even.'

'You have to ask them,' Dev said. The tingling in his

jaws intensified. Saliva welled in his throat. He swallowed, carefully. 'If they said OK—'

A low growl of frustration escaped Doll's throat.

'They said they've been talking to your brother,' Dev said. 'It's going to get sorted.'

He sensed movement out of the corner of his eye and looked to the window. The Ferdias were moving back up towards the house.

'What's going to happen?' Doll pleaded.

'I don't know,' Dev said.

'How can you not know?'

'None of this was my business until they landed here with you.'

'Why are you going along with it?'

'I'm not.'

'You're keeping me here on those two cunts' say-so.'

'I'm not keeping you anywhere.'

'You are, man. You're doing it, too. Your oul fella was cracked in the head and probably didn't have the where-withal to even know what he was doing, but you do, man. You can shuffle around all you want looking sad and say-ing next to nothing but you're all there and you know what you're doing. '

Dev stepped back against the counter, felt the telltale shiver on his neck. He closed his eyes and the silver motes surged and proliferated in a whirl. His head began to spin. His chest tightened like a fist.

The shunting open of the back door and the Ferdias came in.

'What's going on?' Dev heard Gabe say.

'Nothing,' Dev said.

'Are you OK?'

'He don't look too fucking hot,' Sketch drawled.

Dev wanted to sit. There was a chair near him. But he thought if he stepped forward to reach it, he might falter or fall. It felt like blades were beating against his chest.

'I'm good,' he managed, his breath tight, 'I'm good.'

'What the fuck is happening?' Gabe said to the kid. 'What did you do?'

'We were just talking,' Doll said.

'About what?'

'Nothing.'

'Nothing? Huh? Nothing,' Gabe said. 'Dev. What happened?'

Even with his eyes open, the silver motes were there, swirling and popping like flashbulbs blowing out, each silver detonation leaving a thrumming black negative in its wake. He was looking right at Gabe and Sketch but he could not make out their faces in this swarm of silver and black flashing.

'He's having a heart attack,' Doll said. 'He's dying.'

'Shut the fuck up,' Gabe said.

Sketch came over to Dev.

'Are you actually dying, man?' he said. He said it softly, with curiosity, and placed a hand on Dev's back and began rubbing in gentle circles.

'I just need a minute,' Dev said.

'What are we going to do?' Sketch said to Gabe.

'Give me a minute,' Dev repeated. He went for the

chair and his knees melted beneath him. Sketch's arm, sure and quick, slid in under his elbow to take his weight.

'You're going to be OK, fella,' Sketch said, steering him into the seat.

Once he was sitting Dev hung his head and shut his eyes tight. A thread of spittle dropped from between his teeth. He found it with his thumb and touched it away.

'He needs an ambulance,' Doll said.

'I think maybe,' Dev said, 'maybe the kid shouldn't be here any more.'

'Come on now, man, you're going to be OK,' Sketch said encouragingly.

Dev heard commotion in front of him.

'Let's go,' he heard Gabe say.

Dev looked up. Gabe was addressing Doll. Doll did not react. Or his non-reaction was his reaction. Gabe grabbed him by the neck of the NEVERMIND T-shirt and wrenched him out of the chair to his feet.

'Let's go,' he repeated and dragged Doll across the room and shoved him into the hall.

'Come on!' Gabe shouted back to Sketch.

'Wait here, lad,' Sketch said and patted Dev on the shoulder.

Georgie pursued the Ferdias and Doll partway down the hall, then turned tail and jogged back to the kitchen. He curled in and out between Dev's legs, barking and barking. Dev heard steps on the stairs. He concentrated on his breathing, on the air coming in slow points through his nose. The ends of his fingers were tingling and cold. He wanted to know what they were going to do to Doll.

But he had to wait for the terrible pounding in his chest to recede; no matter how many times it happened, each time felt like the first time.

After a few minutes, he was able to get up and make his way down the hall, a hand on the wall to steady himself.

As he climbed the stairs he could hear the thick, resonant sound of water crashing into water. The bathroom door was ajar. The Ferdias and the kid were crammed in there. Dev pulled the door back and stepped in, further crowding the space. The floor was drenched. Steam was clouding the air. Doll was on his knees between Gabe and Sketch, head soaked and dripping, his top dark and clinging to him in sodden ribbons. The tub was filled with water, a big bowled mass of it densely wobbling and more water pummelling down from the spigot. Gabe glanced in the direction of Dev, his eyes hot and indiscriminate. He grit his jaw, firmed his grasp on Doll's shoulder and neck, and pitched him head first into the tub. Water crashed in every direction, flurried spatters hitting the walls and slices of water flopping heavily out over the lip of the tub, drenching the already drenched floor. Doll's head was completely under the water. Gabe pushed Doll further into the bath and climbed up on top of him, knee on his back to keep him in place. Dev watched Doll's legs scrambling, the soles of his runners squeaking frenetically for purchase on the shining tiles. Gabe was pressing down so intensely on Doll he was almost in the water himself.

Sketch was just standing there, watching.

Dev stepped forward.

Sketch came out of his spectating trance.

'Get out to fuck,' he snarled and shoved Dev in the shoulder.

Dev faltered back a step.

He went to say something, but his throat clenched up.

Doll was still under the water.

Gabe's forehead was swelling and buckling with the tremendous unceasing effort of holding him down, of keeping him under the water. The simple, clear thought came to Dev that if Gabe did not let Doll up, then Doll was going to drown. This thought amazed him in its starkness and surety. It amazed him that the kid was going to drown because Gabe would not let him up. But it was going to happen, and happen right here, in Dev's house.

Without thinking about it, as if submitting to a mechanical impulse, Dev stepped into the centre of the room and placed a hand on Gabe's shoulder. *Excavator buckets.* He pulled Gabe back, not even too hard, with just enough force to drag the man off balance. Gabe wavered and staggered back on the wet floor, his footing sliding around under him. Doll reared up out of the bath and fell back onto the floor with a splash.

'What the fuck did I say?' Sketch yelled, grabbing Dev by the arm. Sketch got his face right in Dev's, teeth bared, the close gleam of his bulging eyes. A sudden charge went through Dev. He thrust his hands forward and watched himself, his own body, hoist Sketch in a single unstoppable sweep up into the air and slam him into the cabinet in a shatter of glass, hundreds of flashing pieces following Sketch to the floor where he landed on his shoulder.

For a moment there was no sound. Nobody spoke.

Doll was lying on his back on the tiles, glistening and sprawl-limbed as a new-born calf. Dev watched the steady buck and drop of his ribcage as his breath paced itself back into his body. There seemed to be water dripping and gleaming on every inch of the wall and the floor. There was a sickly, acidic taint to the air.

Gabe was standing with a hand against the wall, catching his breath. His face was flushed, and Dev could see the sweat crawling in runnels out of his scalp, the furious ticking of a vein in the brow of his eye. His face was glowing red and sweat-sheened, that same ragged, playing-card flicker buried in the underdraw of his long, deep breaths. His eyes were closed. He looked almost asleep on his feet.

Sketch sat up. Around him lay a bristling moat of scattered toiletries and mirror shards. There were spatters of blood on his arms. He set himself back against the wall and turned a forearm in the air, following the trail of blood tracing a path along his limb back to its source. He looked up and caught Dev's eye.

'Who knew you had it in you?' he said with a wide-eyed, marvelling smile.

PART THREE

9

Nicky was standing on the middle bridge over the Moy, elbows resting on the stone lip of the wall. It was Monday, a little after nine in the morning. She was drinking a coffee and biting fitfully at her nails, a steady trickle of cars coming along the quays. Ahead of her, some distance upstream, the weir gates were slitted open, and the noise the river made as it crashed through the gates was like meat sizzling on a grill.

On the embankment below the bridge, two men were watching a third reel in a fish. Nicky knew next to nothing about fishing, but she knew the Moy was thronged with salmon, hence the festival, hence the fishers out here, all day every day. The third man was knee-deep in the water and reversing slowly, the struggling fish surfacing and disappearing, until the man stepped up onto the embankment. The fish dangled in the air. The man tore it from the line, belted the shimmering muscle of it twice against the embankment wall and tossed it into an ice box.

Nicky slipped her thumb into her mouth and eased the

stub of a hangnail off, drawing a tiny tang of blood. The blood spread warm and sweet in her mouth. She took a draw of her coffee. It was bitter and lukewarm, already her third of the morning. She was not due into the Pearl until ten but she'd been awake since six. Out and driving around just like yesterday, going out of her mind about Doll, about what Sheila had asked her to do. She'd barely slept last night, or the night before.

On the Saturday night, after the incident at the bar, Nicky's first instinct had been to go to Sheila, not Cillian. She drove straight to the English house. A startled, groggy Sheila, no glasses and an eye mask pushed up onto her forehead, let her inside.

'I've news about Doll.'

'Doll's not here,' Sheila said confusedly.

'I know,' Nicky said.

They sat at the kitchen table, teas steaming in front of them, as Nicky told Sheila about the man in the Pearl. As she spoke, Nicky faced the window onto the backyard. In the glass she could see nothing but a perfect yellow duplicate of the kitchen floating in a black void. It was strange. Instead of becoming emotional and jumping in, as Nicky assumed she would, Sheila did not interject or question anything Nicky said. She just sat in her seat, drawing one hand repeatedly through the cinch of the other and listening with grave raptness, right up until Nicky mentioned Cillian's name. Then she jerked and moaned in her seat, like she'd been struck.

'Cillian,' she said. 'Cillian, Cillian, Cillian.'

Sheila told Nicky they had to go to Glen Gardens, right

now. Nicky drove them and stood there behind Sheila as she pounded on the front door and shouted his name until Cillian opened it. She put her hands on his chest and pushed him straight back into the hall.

'Ma, what's wrong?' he said, catching her wrists to hold her in place, for once looking completely surprised, for once sounding helplessly in earnest.

'You will sort this now,' Sheila declared and stormed into the sitting room. The room was the usual mess, duvet spread across the couch, the cavity made by Cillian's body visible in its wrenched-back folds. On the coffee table the ordered circle of the rock garden was surrounded on all sides by a detritus of popped beer cans, cigarette papers, torn wrappers, food scraps.

Nicky watched Sheila take in this sight. She wondered when Sheila had last been here. She wondered if she was appalled, or if Cillian's life conformed exactly to what she had imagined.

'Sort what now?' Cillian said.

'Do you know where Doll is?' Sheila said.

'I don't.'

'He wasn't home today,' Sheila said, 'or last night.'

'I don't know where that lad has elected to take himself, but he's not here,' Cillian said, not meeting Sheila's eye, pushing away the duvet and taking a seat on the couch.

'Oh, I know that,' Sheila said.

In the hall, there was the sound of steps on the stairs, then Sara Duane joined them in the sitting room. She was in a pink robe, her hair down. Wincing against the light, she took in Sheila and Nicky.

'What's wrong?' she said. 'Is everything OK?'

'Go on,' Sheila said to Nicky, ignoring Sara. 'Tell him what you told me.'

Cillian looked at Nicky with a reflexive flash of resentment, like he was just noticing her for the first time.

'I was working in the Pearl this evening when this fella comes in,' Nicky began. 'He takes a seat up at the bar, starts on the pints. Sketchy enough vibe, the kind of fella you're happy to leave to his own devices. About eleven, I head into one of the back rooms to do a bit of a clean-up, and that same fella follows me in. He corners me and tells me he's a message for you, hits me a dig in the leg so I don't forget it.'

'What's the message?' Cillian said, his voice choked with dawning knowledge.

'He said they have Doll. That they have Doll staying with them, and he'll keep staying with them, until you get what you owe them. He said you have until Monday, and they are going to call you tomorrow and when they ring you better pick up.'

'What is this, Cillian?' Sheila said.

He sat upright, dialled a number and held his phone tight to his ear.

'We've been trying that,' Sheila said.

After it rang out, Cillian dropped the phone from his ear. He looked at the phone again, considering.

'This fella give you a name by any chance?' he said.

'He said you'd know him,' Nicky said. 'He called you a cunt, if that helps.'

'Yeah, it does,' Cillian said. 'What he look like?'

'I don't know. He was in his forties, maybe. Tall enough, skinny, browny-red hair.'

'Did he have an ugly fucking dug-out rat's face on him?'

'He was rough enough looking.'

'And he was on his own? You're sure?'

'I didn't see no one with him. He'd a jacket, said "Tequila Patrol" on the back.'

'Fuck's sake. Tequila Patrol,' Cillian snarled. 'That fucking prick. Tell me what he said, exactly.'

'*We have Doll. Doll is staying with us and he's gonna keep staying with us until Cillian gets us what he owes us,*' Nicky said.

'Cillian,' Sheila said, 'who do you owe, and what do you owe them?'

'This is my problem, Mother,' he said.

'Oh, fuck you, Cillian,' Sheila said with sudden anger. She groped for the arm of the chair behind her and descended carefully into the seat. 'You hope it's a terrible cod,' she said. 'A bad joke. Tell me what is going on, Cillian.'

'Cillian,' Sara entreated him, 'tell them.'

He hesitated for a moment, perhaps expecting his mother to start in on him again, but she just stared at him, her expression resolute, scornfully undivulging.

'About a year back, the crowd I was working with,' he began, 'they needed someone local to start holding things here for them, stuff they were moving through the region. I said I could do that, no problem.'

'Stuff,' Sheila said.

Cillian tiredly rubbed the corner of his eye.

'Drugs,' he said, 'you know that.'

'I do.' She grimaced. 'Go on.'

'I needed somewhere to keep the stuff and I had this spot, way out in Belleek Wood, in a part of the park closed off to the public. It was this hidden away little cave, narrow and deep. A crack in the ground basically, buried under a big pile of brush, far off any track. I was keeping bits of my own stuff there, wrapped up tight and safe against animals and the weather and all that, and it had all been grand to that point. So that's where I stashed the stuff I was holding for this other crowd.'

Cillian stopped. He took out a cigarette, stared at it as if he was about to light it. An unhappy smile crossed his face.

'You know what a turlough is?' he asked.

'Enlighten me,' Sheila said.

'Not far from the spot I was using there was a sort of open field, really just a long, flat stretch of grass, then more trees and brush and not much else. Only one day, coming into winter, I head out to the spot and as I come up to it I see there's a lake right where that field should be. The whole area under water. And my spot, too. I go back later that day with Rubber Nallin and a length of rope and nearly drowned trying to get down to the gear. Not a hope. Rubber reckoned it was flash-flooding, said it would go down in a day or two, only it didn't. When I was finally able to get to it everything was gone, the whole stash, dissolved away to nothing. The lake stayed there for weeks, then it just drained away. And that's what a turlough is. A seasonal fucking lake.'

'A turlough,' Sheila said bewilderedly.

'A turlough,' Cillian repeated. 'Ireland's the only place in the world they exist. And the West is the only place in Ireland they exist. A turlough, a magical fucking lake sprang up out of nowhere and drank thirty grand of coke on me.'

'Thirty grand.'

'Yeah.'

'How could you be so stupid?' Sheila said and her posture slackened, just a fraction, in her seat. She was still wearing her nightclothes under her coat – a faded T-shirt and sweatpants. Her finely stranded hair, the grey coming through the brown dye, was tousled, awry. She screwed up her eyes and glanced at the light in the centre of the ceiling, rooted in her pocket and took out her dark glasses. She put them on and looked straight at her son.

'Give them their money,' she said with cold measuredness.

'I don't have it.'

'Cillian. They have Doll. You need to give them their money.'

'I don't have it to give to them.'

'He paid them what he could already,' Sara said. 'He's paid them almost half. He's cleaned himself out paying what he could.'

'They wouldn't believe me when I told them what happened,' Cillian said, 'or they think I fucked them over, took the stuff myself to sell it on the sly. They cut me off, won't give me anything to make the rest back. I've had nothing coming in since. I'm on the dole, for fuck's sake.'

Sheila came up out of the chair. She began to circle the room.

'Cillian, tell me,' she said, her voice edged now with a

rising urgency. 'Tell me and don't mess with me: how are you going to sort this? It's Doll they have. Your little brother. How are you going to get Doll back?'

Nicky watched Cillian's face. He was watching his mother, eyes following her in her circling, with a dreadful longing. His eyes had turned dark and large, expressively large, like a kid's, the rings beneath them a greasy, water-logged blue.

'I don't know,' he said.

'You have to get him back,' Sheila said, coming close to him.

'I know,' he said, 'I know.'

'YOU IDIOT, YOU STUPID, STUPID FUCK-ING IDIOT,' Sheila roared. She began slapping furiously at him. Cillian raised his arm, not so much to ward her off as to easier accept her blows.

'Sheila, please!' Sara pleaded. Nicky wondered if she should intervene, hold Sheila back. But neither she nor Sara did anything as Sheila continued to rain down blows, wholehearted but feeble, on Cillian. Presently Sheila did stop, stalked back to her chair, turned as if to fling herself into it, and then just stood there, glaring at her son. She seemed to be caught in an agony of contending impulses, every prospective course of action, including its opposite, rendered intolerable the instant she considered it.

'Doll is innocent of all this . . . shit,' she hissed, 'this world of shit you've elected to live in.'

'I know,' Cillian said.

Sheila looked at Nicky. Nicky could see the angry gloss of tears in her eyes.

'And this poor young one, in at work, getting threatened on your behalf.'

'This is meant to be between me and them,' Cillian said. 'Doll had nothing to do with it.'

'These shitheads are meant to be his friends!' Sara exclaimed. 'He was always the one running the risk for them. He's paid every cent he could so far. He can't sleep over it. I can barely get him to eat. All they had to do was give him time—'

'You have to do something about this, Cillian,' Sheila said. 'You can't just sit here.'

'I know,' he said. 'I will.'

Sheila looked for a moment as if she might attack him again. Then her gaze ranged about the room, as if there might be some other presence, some hitherto concealed third party, to whom she could appeal, with whom she could negotiate. But there was no one.

'All these years,' she said to Cillian. 'All these years thinking that underneath it all, you might be more than what you are. Wasn't I the fool.'

By the time Nicky got back to the apartment it was three in the morning. She crawled into bed, phone propped on her pillow at eye level, watching it, willing Doll's number to appear. She must have slept, came to with a start at dawn still in her work clothes, light gathering in the window, the shades of which she'd forgotten to draw.

She did not know what else to do, so she took the car out. She drove to Foxford and then over to Castlebar, out to Westport, back up and around Newport, Mulranny,

Crossmolina. She drove through towns, villages, housing estates. She took random turn-offs down narrow country lanes, crawled to a halt outside lone houses and stared hard at their front windows, small and darkly indecipherable as photo negatives. She imagined improvised cells behind the rickety, bolt-locked barnyard doors glimpsed at the ends of boreens.

Nicky drove without hope, burning through an anxious and dwindling sense of compulsion. The countryside was huge and quiet and empty, and for every road she took, she had to forgo a dozen others, all those byways and back roads that digressed for miles into further orders of rural obscurity. Doll was lost and she needed to find him but the countryside wasn't giving her anything; the countryside was holding its tongue and steadfastly averting its gaze as she travelled towards the unending low horizon and the indistinct serrations of the distant mountain ranges, the wide-open fields flipping by like the row of blank pages at the end of a book after the story was over.

In the afternoon, she parked in a forecourt outside Charlestown and drank a smoothie sitting on the bonnet of her car. As she did so, a minibus with an illustration of a demonically grinning leprechaun raising a pint decaled onto the side of it pulled in, and she watched an assortment of lads – they had the ashen complexions, crumpled collars and ransacked postures of fellas the other side of a stag weekend – file into the petrol station and then back out, each clutching a medicinal chicken salad roll and energy drink which they collectively housed right there on the tarmac while the minibus driver smoked a cigarette and stared diplomatically off into the distance. Nicky had almost wanted to cry at the sight of these men, so safely ensconced in the ordinariness of their dismal, hungover Sunday. Then she drove back to Ballina and went into work because what else could she do?

The Sunday-evening crowd was not quite as big as Saturday's, but there was still a fervour to the air in the Pearl, more than enough to keep her preoccupied, even if several times some fella with a redolently wiry frame and bony face appeared at the end of the bar and made her jump in her skin.

Then Sheila called. Nicky missed the call, but when she next got the opportunity, locked herself in a staff toilet and called her back.

'Sorry to bother you now, Nicky,' Sheila said, her voice low but steady. 'Only I was thinking about this situation we are in, and something occurred to me. Can I tell you what it is?'

'You can,' Nicky said.

'Years ago, when I wasn't much older than you, I worked in a pub out on the Foxford road. The Yellow Thistle. It's gone years now. It's where I first met Doll's father, for my sins. But what I was thinking about today was how several times a year – during Christmas and the holidays and whatnot – we'd always get a big crowd in, and often we would end up with double or even treble the takings for the week.'

'OK,' Nicky said.

'The takings would go out on a Monday. Usually the morning. One of the lads would just pack it up and drive the money over the bank.'

Sheila paused again, as if waiting for Nicky to say something, but she did not.

'And that's what I was wondering, Nicky,' Sheila continued after a moment. 'If the takings in the Pearl go out on a Monday?'

The answer was yes, but Nicky wavered about saying so.

'I'm awful worried about my son, Nicky,' Sheila urged. 'I'm worried about Doll.'

Nicky nodded in agreement, as if Sheila could see her. Nicky imagined sitting in the English kitchen with Doll and Sheila, drinking tea and eating biscuits and just talking, as they had countless times over the course of Nicky and Doll's relationship. During these conversations, Sheila would often ask Nicky a series of occasionally pointed questions about some aspect of her life. And if this exact same conversation were occurring at her kitchen table, with Sheila pursuing just this line of questioning, then Nicky wouldn't have thought twice about answering her, because nothing she could tell her was any kind of secret.

'They do,' she said finally. 'The takings. Usually, they go out on a Monday.'

'What time would they go out? Early?'

'Not too early,' Nicky said. 'He's a bit lax about it, these days.'

'And who's that, now? What's the manager fella's name again?'

'Flynn.'

'And what time, roughly, would Flynn bring the takings out?'

'Different times.'

'But roughly, what time, would you say? The morning, I'd say.'

'The morning, sometimes later. Eleven, noonish,' Nicky said, 'in and around lunchtime, because Flynn will usually get his lunch in town after.'

'And he takes it in his own car, I suppose? That's what the lad always used to do in the Thistle.'

'He does, yeah.'

'What kind of car does this Flynn lad drive?'

'Like, an Audi.'

'They're all very drab colours, cars these days. What's his? Grey? White?'

'It's white, yeah.'

'Well, there you go,' Sheila said. Then she said something Nicky didn't catch. The din of the pub was beginning to seep through the toilet door.

'What?' Nicky said, pressing the palm of her hand against her exposed ear and crouching down to hear Sheila better.

'I said I'm in the grip of it now. A full-bore migraine. Squeezing down on me. It's a bad one, Nicky. I didn't get a wink of sleep last night.'

'Me either.'

'I just want Doll home.'

'That's what I want too,' Nicky said.

'I know you do,' Sheila said. 'Thank you, love.'

Nicky took her finger out of her mouth and examined the gnawed spot where she'd bitten off the hangnail. The flesh was torn and still stinging but the blood had stopped. She could not believe what Sheila might have recruited her into. A part of her did want to say something to Flynn. Not even anything overt, just come up with some reason for him to postpone heading off with the takings later today. But every time she thought about potentially doing that, Nicky remembered that that man had given Cillian a deadline of Monday, and so whatever it was that needed to happen, needed to happen today. She finished her coffee. She bit her nails. She kept checking her phone until it was time to go.

Work was quiet when Nicky got in. There were several guests having breakfast in the restaurant. Barry Madigan was behind the bar, on his phone. Madigan was in his late forties. He played keyboards in a band. He was tall, with a massive, protuberant forehead like an alien and a woeful arrangement of hair – thin on top and raked back in wide-spaced furrows, the ratty remnant of a ponytail dangling between his shoulder blades. He was sound. He made little to no effort with the job and had somehow never been fired. Nicky reckoned Flynn kept him around just so there was someone he could reliably give out to and about. Nicky headed onto the floor. After a while Flynn appeared. He went straight in behind the bar, took a glass off the shelf, held it to the light, rotated it, checked a second glass. He said something short and no doubt sharp to Madigan, then came out onto the floor and over to the greeting station. At the greeting station there was a stand and a table bearing a spray of synthetic white orchids lolling in a vase, a stack of menus, scrolled napkins, a jug of water and a metal pail of sweating ice cubes. Flynn chunked a scoopful of the ice into the glass, poured a water. He sipped, ran his tongue over his teeth, and made a face, all the time watching Nicky as she finished a circuit of the room.

'Don't serve that,' he said when Nicky came over to the greeting station. 'You can taste tap off that. Who said to serve that?'

'I'm only in the door,' Nicky said.

Flynn passed her the glass.

'Taste it. Go on.'

She took a sip.

'You getting that taste?'

She took another sip, duplicated Flynn's action of running the water around her teeth. It didn't taste like anything. It tasted fine.

'Is that the water or the ice though?' she said, just to say something.

'Never mind the ice,' Flynn said. 'I taste water like that in any place serving food at our price points, I'm not coming back. It doesn't have to be Evian. It just can't be tap.'

'Talk to Barry.'

'I'll talk to fucking Barry,' Flynn said with severity. 'You understand why though.'

'It's not good enough,' she said.

'Comped water,' Flynn said. 'It's the easiest thing in the world not to fuck up.'

Flynn left and it was just Nicky and Madigan minding the bar and floor. The manager's office was in the hall just off the restaurant. At some point, Flynn would enter the office, count out and bundle up the money before packing the lot into the raggedy canvas satchel he always used – it must have been Flynn's old school bag – and head out to his car to transport it to the bank, just like Nicky had told Sheila he would. Not long after eleven she saw Flynn step inside and close the door behind him. Nicky's heart started beating fast. There was a window, diminishing second by second, in which she might still contrive to persuade Flynn not to run the takings into town. Then she thought of Doll and all she could do was continue to walk the floor in a near daze, wiping down already clean tables, tucking chairs into place. A little while later, Flynn came back out of the office, the bag slung over his shoulder.

Nicky caught up with him.

'I've to tell you something,' she said, offering a smile as she walked alongside him, steeling herself to be friendly.

'What's that now?' Flynn said distractedly.

'I've failed again. I'm back on the smokes. Fancy one?'

'I'm about to head.'

'Only I don't have any cigarettes,' Nicky said. 'I figure if you have a quick one now, I can bum one off you.'

Flynn slowed up. He frowned and submitted a quick, apprehensive lick of the lips. She knew he was going to give in.

'I'm trying to give them up myself too,' he said, 'just so you know.'

'Trying not to smoke and having a smoke,' Nicky said, 'is still trying.'

The spot where they smoked was at the back of the car park, next to the low wall that ran along the Moy. On the other side of the wall scrubby formations of rock and a succession of skinny trees sloped down to the water. There was enough of a wind kicking in off the river to twice dash the flame of Flynn's lighter before he could spark up.

'Little help,' he said.

She hooked a flickering strand of hair out of the corner of her mouth, drew it back over her ear, and took the lighter. Flynn uptilted his chin and tensed his jaw to keep the cigarette level. Nicky lifted the flame towards his face, and as she did, Flynn brought his hands up on either side of hers to form a screen from the elements, close, but taking care not to touch her.

'What time you on to tonight?' he asked her once her cigarette was lit too.

'Six.'

'You'll have an evening to enjoy, so.'

'Just about.'

'What'll that entail?'

'Not much, I reckon. An early night, probably.'

'Why's a young one like you not out on the tear tonight?'

'It's Monday. Young ones aren't always out on the tear, you know.'

'I was.'

'Good for you,' Nicky said, trying to appear casual as she scanned the car park. It was half full, maybe twenty vehicles on the premises, and more cars parked along the road just outside the entrance. Here is where Cillian would do it, she reckoned, if he was going to.

'How's himself?' Flynn said to her.

'Doll?'

'Doll.' Flynn grinned. 'No offence, I can't believe the sham you're going out with is called Doll.'

'I forget sometimes,' she said. 'To me it's just his name, now. People say it suits him.'

'Maybe it does,' Flynn said.

A car entered the car park and started coming in their direction, gleaming patches of sky reeling in the windscreen. The car was moving slowly, but that's how cars moved in car parks. Nicky looked out over the water as it passed them by, and when she looked back, the car was concluding a lap of the car park and was almost back at the exit.

'You'll be back in school in no time,' Flynn said.

'It's a while away, yet,' Nicky said.

'You still have to give me the date you intend finishing up here.'

'No, I will,' she said.

'We'll miss you,' he said. 'You're one of the only ones in here with a head on your shoulders.'

Nicky looked at him.

'Am I?' she said.

'Once you're back in school you might have your plate full, but if you wanted to keep doing a few hours on the weekends, we can sort that, if you want. And if you wanted to come back full-time next summer, I can get you back on the books. That's not going to be a problem.'

'Thanks.'

'Because you're a good worker.'

The car had come to a halt at the exit. It was just waiting there, indicator flashing, preparing to turn out onto the main road.

'You said that before,' she said to Flynn.

'What?'

'That I've a head on my shoulders.'

'I did?'

'Yeah, you did.'

He adjusted the strap of the satchel on his shoulder.

'Well, if I did,' he said, 'I meant it then, and I mean it now.'

That was enough to do it, to revive in Nicky the sour, circling feeling of the night of the bike rally, the grinding small talk and the final feeble intrusion of Flynn's kiss. She took a step back. The car was still up at the exit. Two seconds went by, three. She could taste the smoke in her mouth and all at once she was aware of the sound of the river, the tremendous bristling static of its flow, so rich and incessant it seemed like a type of silence. She watched the indicator flashing on, off, on. Nothing was happening, except what was happening.

'You all right?' Flynn said.

Nicky looked at him and smiled emptily. Her heart was racing. The car could be any car. The second she ended this conversation he would get in his car and head to the bank, that was all.

'OK,' she said coldly, tossing the cigarette to the ground and stamping on it. 'I'd better get back to it.'

She turned and strode to the service door. She pushed the door in and stepped inside and only then did she look back. Flynn was already over at his car. She watched him pop the boot, the lid floating up as he unshouldered the satchel. As he did so, there was the sharp growl of an engine and the car at the exit lurched out onto the road, turned and came barrelling back into the car park. A wave of feeling – it was shock, but a sick kind of gratified shock – surged through her with such dizzying intensity it almost spun her off her feet. She leaned in against the door like she was drunk, closing it to a crack. Through the sliver of space, she watched the car squeal to a halt a few feet short of Flynn, who just stood there with the satchel in his arms, in frozen incomprehension, as the door swung open and a man, his face covered, jumped out. The masked man took two steps towards Flynn and in the span of those two steps Nicky could see the cockeyed slant to his shoulders. A part of Nicky did want to shout, but her throat shied as the clear, hard thought came to her that she needed to be able to tell anyone who later asked that she saw nothing. Clutching the handle tight, tight enough that her hand would not shake, she closed the door slowly, listening for the lock to click into place before releasing the handle as carefully as if she were letting go of the bladed end of a knife.

10

Dev fetched towels from the press on the landing. As Doll dried off, Dev went to drain the bath and saw that Doll had thrown up in it; gobs of half-digested meat and the odd intact bean had settled amid the cloudy petroleum swirl of whatever else his belly had disgorged.

Dev got Doll to help clean up the wrecked bathroom. They swept up and bagged the broken glass, mopped the floor, scoured the tub. Doll remained obedient and quiet as they worked, speaking only when spoken to. Anything Dev directed him to do was done without a hint of dissension or mouth.

Dev noticed again the raw, blistered state of Doll's wrists.

'Here, I've cream in the medicine box,' he told him once they had done what they could to tidy the bathroom.

They went downstairs.

The Ferdias were in the kitchen, drinking Coronas at the table, their clothing still blotched with damp patches.

When Dev led Doll in, the brothers turned their attention upon them without remark.

Dev brought down the medicine box. He took hold of one of Doll's wrists, applied and kneaded in the disinfectant cream, did the second wrist. Doll sighed through his teeth but did not complain or resist. Dev popped two paracetamol from their foil packaging and ran a glass of water, all the time cognisant of the Ferdias' brooding scrutiny.

'Here,' he said, handing the pills to Doll.

'Have you a plaster there, Dev?' Sketch said. He lifted his arm to indicate the fresh thread of blood trickling down his forearm. Dev rooted out a plaster and brought it over to Sketch.

'See how lucky you are, now,' Gabe said, saluting Doll with his Corona.

Doll said nothing.

'The trouble you'd be in if it wasn't for Dev,' Gabe continued. 'What you need to start doing is showing him a modicum of respect.'

'He's right there now,' Sketch agreed, peeling the cellophane strip off and slapping the plaster onto his arm.

Doll's eyes had a lifeless opaque shine, like marbles.

'C'mon,' Dev said.

They went into the sitting room. Dev directed Doll onto the sofa.

'Want to watch something? There's rakes on the hard drive,' Dev said, scrolling through the library. 'Could watch something funny, or?'

He looked over at Doll.

'You seen *Superbad*?' he tried.

No response, no acknowledgement of Dev's question. Dev pitched the remote at Doll's head, aiming just off centre at the last moment. The remote winged Doll's shoulder, rebounded off the wall and dropped back down onto the sofa, the batteries popping from the back at the impact. Still no reaction.

'For fuck's sake,' Dev hissed, stooping to retrieve the batteries from the floor. He picked one up and it skipped out of his fingers and rolled under the sofa. 'For fuck's sake, for fuck's sake,' he said, getting down on his knees and groping in under the sofa, his cheeks burning with remorse and tears of frustration filming his eyes. When he looked up, Doll was still staring vacantly at the TV screen.

'I'll watch whatever,' he mumbled.

Around ten Sketch appeared at the sitting-room door and said it was time for the kid to go down. Dev wanted to say something about his wrists. Was it necessary to tie him up? Could they do it a different way? Tie him by his legs or something, just to relieve his wrists for a night. As he thought about this, he saw that Sketch was eyeing him, his look sidelong and intransigent, like he knew what Dev was thinking and was ready to light on him if he so much as said a word. So Dev said nothing, just watched Doll get up and go off with Sketch.

Dev sat there for a while, the TV going. He did not know how much time had passed before he snapped it off. The pain in his head was there again, mild and diffuse. Sometimes he wondered if it ever truly went away, or if it was just that it intermittently dulled enough to permit him to stop noticing it.

He entered the kitchen. Georgie was asleep in the basket by the back door, eyes closed but his nose pointed raptly up and one hind leg lifted a little from his body, gently kick-starting the air as he dreamt whatever it is dogs dream of. The kitchen table was by now covered in drained Corona bottles. The Ferdias had resorted to the last of the Baileys. They were drinking it out of teacups. Dev brought the medicine box out of its cabinet. Only two paracetamol left in the pack. He popped them.

'Your mother used to take this with ice?' Gabe said abruptly, nodding at the bottle of Baileys. The glass of the bottle was so dark you could not see through it.

'She did,' Dev said.

'That's the thing,' Gabe said with a gloating click of the tongue. 'You're meant to refrigerate Baileys. Because of the cream. The liquor doesn't go off, but the cream does. You keep it chilled, you drink it chilled. Keeping it at room temperature and then adding ice at the last; it's too late in the equation.'

'So she was doing it wrong all these years,' Dev said.

'She wouldn't have been the first.'

'As long as it gets you where you need to go, who gives a shite?' Sketch said with gruff diplomacy as he downed his cupful.

'Sorry,' Gabe said, 'sorry, sorry, sorry,' he chanted, looking at Dev, stretching and squeezing out the word, extruding it into a taunt. 'That's what I wanted to say. SORRY I lost my composure earlier.'

He wiped the corner of his mouth with the back of his hand. He was at least a little drunk.

For a moment, Dev did consider asking Gabe why he had done what he had done. Had he really intended to drown Doll? Or just scare him? Would he have let Doll up of his own accord had Dev not intervened? But he knew there was no point. Without even taking into account the near certainty that Gabe would simply lie through his teeth, the likeliest answer the man could give to any of these questions was that he did not know; that, swept up in the moment, he had dragged Doll upstairs and held his head under water and would have kept doing so until the surge of temper coursing through him had begun to abate. By which point, Doll would, or would not, have been dead. The Ferdias had the unreliability, but also the dangerous decisiveness, of creatures who did not understand their nature and did not care to understand it. You could never tell what lines they would elect to cross, what courses of action they would follow through to the bitter end, because they did not know either.

'Only I got a bit riled up there, when I came in here to the kitchen and saw the state of you,' Gabe said. 'You can't blame me for assuming the kid must have said something to put you in that state.'

'We did think you we're having a heart attack, man,' Sketch said.

Dev folded his arms. This was the tack they were trying now. Putting it on that they had been acting out of concern for him.

'What the kid said had nothing to do with it,' Dev said. 'I told you I wasn't having a heart attack.'

'If it wasn't a heart attack, what the fuck was it, man?' Sketch said.

Dev marvelled at the swiftness with which they had moved the topic on to him, how brusquely they had cornered him with their talk.

'I get spells,' Dev said.

'Spells.'

'Like, light-headed. Like a dizzy and sick feeling. My chest gets at me.'

'Like a panic attack,' Sketch said.

'Something like that.'

Gabe and Sketch looked at him.

'It comes and goes,' Dev said.

'How long's it been coming and going?' Gabe said.

'I suppose . . .' Dev said, 'once the mother went. Maybe it's been at me a bit more since.'

'Well, Jesus now, Dev,' Gabe muttered and for a moment he seemed almost taken aback, 'you could have enlightened us.'

'It's my business.'

'I'm afraid it's our business too, lad. Given the ongoing arrangement between you and Mulrooney.'

'You have to tell us about these things, Dev,' Sketch put in.

'This is my house,' Dev said, carefully but clearly. 'Don't be telling me what I have to do in my house.'

'The thing about you, Dev,' Gabe said, 'you're a straight shooter. That's what I told Mulrooney back when I recommended you. There'll be no conniving out of Dev,

I told him, no skulduggery. What you see is what you'll get.'

'I need to know when this is going to be done with,' Dev said.

Gabe cleared his throat.

'Tomorrow,' he said. 'Word's been sent to Cillian. He's been told he has to get us the money by tomorrow night.'

'And you reckon he will?'

'He has to.'

He has to, or what? Dev wanted to say. But his fear was that the Ferdias themselves did not know the answer to that.

'How much does he even owe?' Dev said, realising he didn't know the figure, had never asked.

'Eighteen grand,' Sketch said.

'Eighteen?'

'What?' Gabe said.

'Nothing,' Dev said. 'Just, I figured it'd be steeper.'

'Eighteen grand's not nothing, lad.'

'No, I mean it's a fair stack of money.'

'The money's one thing. The bigger thing is the principle of it.'

'The principle,' Dev said.

'The principle,' Gabe repeated, pouring out the last of the Baileys for Sketch and then himself, turning the heavy dark bottle in the air until it was completely inverted, the final few drops dripping from the neck into his teacup.

'So what did he say to you?' he said.

'What?' Dev said.

'The kid. You said *whatever he said had nothing to do with it*. So, he did say something to you. What was it?'

'Nothing,' Dev said.

'No deceiving, Dev.'

'What he said w-was,' Dev stammered, 'he said he met my oul fella.'

'The kid met your oul fella?' Sketch said. 'When?'

'Met him Friday.'

'You're kidding me.'

'Said he was at the hospital on Friday and that's where he met him.'

Gabe and Sketch exchanged glances.

'The hospital?' Sketch said.

'Must have been before we got eyes on him at Cillian's,' Gabe said.

'Or it's bollocks,' Sketch said. He looked at Dev: 'And he's just fucking with you.'

'I don't think he was fucking with me.'

'Why not?'

'Just, the way he described the way he was going on. It sounded like the oul fella.'

'And how was he going on?'

'He said the oul fella asked him to go to the bookies and put a bet on the dogs for him,' Dev said, 'and that's a thing he does. Enlist people to go put a bet on for him, on account he doesn't like going down the town himself.'

Sketch lifted his arm and thumbed the plaster he had just applied, his jaw clenched in thought.

'Oh, I don't like that now,' he said. 'There's no call for you to be telling us that.'

'You told me to tell you,' Dev said.

'We're at a delicate juncture here, lad,' Gabe warned him.

'It was a coincidence.'

'I don't need to hear about any coincidences involving your fucked-in-the-head Guard father meeting that kid, you stupid fucking ape,' Sketch said with sudden violence.

Georgie stirred in his basket, slurred out a dreaming yelp and settled again.

Dev was standing with his tailbone resting on the counter. He gripped the counter's edge and counted in his head to five. He took in a breath and pushed it out his nose.

'I'm not an ape,' he said quietly.

He thought Sketch might light on him again but instead the man sat up in his seat and began rubbing in a sorry fashion at the corner of his jaw, like he'd just been slapped.

'How often do you even see your oul fella, any more?' Gabe said.

'I don't,' Dev said.

'You said he doesn't come around here any more.'

'He doesn't.'

'And you don't go see him?'

'No.'

'The poor fucker's locked up in an institute within in Ballina, and you don't ever go see him?' Sketch said.

The last time Dev had seen his father was the day of the burial. Martin Hendrick materialised halfway through the service in something resembling a mourning suit. The grey trousers did not quite match the black suit jacket. There was someone from the Units with him, an attendant or nurse, some lad in his twenties chewing gum with arrant indifference. They must have put the father on some amount of drugs to get him through the day; in the pub after the service, he moved about in a tranquillised shuffle, and spent most of the time tucked away in corners, staring glassily into space and barely responding to the handful of mourners who approached him to offer the tersest of condolences before returning him to the custody of his gum-chewing chaperone. At one point Dev looked over and saw that his father was alone at the end of the bar. The nurse must have gone to the toilet or off to make a call. There was something on his chin. Dev stepped closer to see.

A translucent stripe of drool had dribbled from the corner of his father's mouth. He did not seem to notice, or if he did, did not care. Up until that point in the day, no unavoidable instance had occurred in which Dev and his father would have had to directly acknowledge or speak to each other, and so they had not; for his part, Dev had not wanted to. He was not sure what, if anything, his half-catatonic father might have wanted.

But now Dev grabbed a couple of napkins and came over to him.

'Here,' he said, waving the napkins at his father.

Martin Hendrick's eyes came slowly onto Dev.

'What?' he said, in a cracked whisper.

Dev indicated his mouth.

'I think you need a—' he said, again proffering the trembling leaves of paper.

'Hah?' was all his father said to that, angling his head and cocking one ear anguishedly at Dev, his whole face contracting into an expression of stricken incomprehension, as if Dev was speaking to him in a language he could not understand, or at a preternaturally low volume, making a noise his father could only partially, and even then only with tremendous inner effort, follow.

'My mother,' Dev said.

All Dev wanted was – some shard, some flicker of acknowledgement. Not for himself, but for her. If Moira Hendrick had given herself completely to Dev she had done the same for this man. The same and more. And for what?

'My mother—' Dev began again.

He choked up.

The breath went out of him like a match.

He could not bear to look at his father. To be anywhere near him. He left the napkins down on the counter and walked away.

Now, in the kitchen of his house, he looked Sketch Ferdia square in the eye.

'No,' he said.

'That's awful fucking cold, man,' Sketch said.

'Don't let him fool you,' Gabe said to his brother. 'There's nothing but ice in this man's veins.'

All Dev wanted to do was go up to bed and be on his own, but the Ferdias reminded him it was his turn on the couch. He took his sleeping pill and brought a blanket down into the sitting room. The day had emptied him out, his nerves warm and dwindling under his skin, like embers in ashes.

That night, he slipped easily into sleep and he did dream. What he dreamt of was his last day in Complere. He had quit right in the middle of a shift. He had intended to wait until the end of the day but all morning his hands had been shaking and he kept having to swallow the ball of sizzling bile continuously rising back into his gullet, so he had stepped into the floor manager Paddy Brogan's office just before lunch and without preamble said he was done as of right now and was leaving and would not be coming back. Brogan looked at him, surprised. He had the big bloodshot eyes and kindly browbeaten features of a bloodhound. Credit to the man, he tried to be sound about it, even though he did not have to be. Caught off guard, he recovered quickly and asked Dev not to make any rash decisions.

After all, it had only been a few months since the mother's passing, Brogan had suggested carefully, and he was sure Dev was still working through that, and he even offered to let Dev take a couple of days' unpaid leave if he wanted, but Dev said no, he'd done all his thinking and his working through it and he had made his decision. He was not going to change his mind.

Dev did agree to return to his station until Brogan was able to get someone in to cover him, then he walked off the floor without further ceremony. He said goodbye to no one, avoiding the eyes of his workmates as he headed straight for the door, though none of them, if they even clocked him leaving, would surely have suspected that he was leaving for good.

Outside, it was high summer and the employee car park

was still and warm in the noonday heat. Dev stood in the cold blue shadow of the factory's corrugated facade and felt no relief. He had not expected to. In the dream, exactly as he had in real life, he sensed the slow, inexorable approach of the shapeless, prospectless days to come, days when there would be no need to get out of bed or brush his teeth or talk to anyone at all, days that would, in time, become unbearable too. For a long moment, he had imagined turning around, going back inside, and telling Brogan that actually he had just made a terrible mistake. But he didn't. It had taken every last scrap of conviction he could muster to drag himself out of bed and make it in that morning. He had only been able to do so because he had sworn to himself he would not have to do it again.

Eventually, with nothing to do and absolutely nowhere to go now but home, he began walking towards the car-park gate. As he passed the ranks of parked cars, the sun struck the slanted surface of each windscreen and flashed in the corner of his eye like a repeating and frantic semaphore. Every time he turned his head to look the light tricked away and he saw that the inside of each car was as dark and empty as a cave.

Monday morning, Dev got up and let Georgie out the back to piss. The weather was calm and dull, the sky a grey wall of cloud faintly backlit by the pale glow of a sun he couldn't see. When he came back inside he got the kid up, applied another round of disinfectant to his wrists. There wasn't much in the fridge. Dev cobbled together a breakfast of toast, tea and boiled eggs.

'How did you sleep?' he asked Doll.

Doll did not answer. There was only the briefest interruption to the rhythm of his chewing before he took a sup of tea and swallowed.

'I think this is all going to be over today,' Dev said. 'Tonight.'

Doll looked at him.

'They got word to Cillian,' Dev went on. 'He's to have the money organised for tonight.'

Doll looked away, over at Georgie, who was lounging peaceably in his basket. Dev watched Doll's jaw tense and ease.

'Today is Monday,' Doll said.

'Yeah.'

'I feel like I been here a long time,' Doll said. He tutted – but not at Dev – and made a sudden gesture with his hand. Georgie sprung out of his basket, trotted over and climbed into the kid's lap. Doll began brushing his hand through Georgie's fur.

'Can I ask you something?' Dev said.

Doll grunted.

'You didn't come here of your own free will.'

'What do you reckon?' Doll scoffed.

'How'd they get you in the car with them?'

'They grabbed me.'

'What happened?'

Doll searched the air with his eyes, weighing up what to say, or if he should say anything at all, perhaps.

'All I was doing was walking an estate road out there by Belleek Wood, head down, doing nothing but minding my own business, when out of nowhere this car pulls up in front of me with an awful screech and the back door swings out. The door was just hanging there, and for a second I didn't know what I was looking at. I thought there must have been a crash or something. Then the Sketch lad slides out across the seat and he's waving his hand at me and saying, *come here, young fella, come here.*'

'I'd've been gone in the other direction, like a shot,' Dev said.

'You get caught cold,' Doll said with a scornful shake of the head. 'You don't even know what's happening and it's already happened. And the thing that fucked me was I half knew the head on him. I would have seen him and the brother hanging around with Cillian over the years. That made me pause. And that pause was all they needed.'

There were wavering little hesitations between each of his sentences, and Dev could see the effort it took, the repeating gull of the head and reset of the shoulders as Doll pushed on through into the next sentence, determined now to get the story all the way out. 'Sketch shoots out and gets a hold of me and starts dragging me into the car. Soon as he has me in, he lands me a shot to the head, straight up with no warning, and the second he done it, he had this grin on him, smiling at me like it was nothing, or like I'd imagined it. He pulls the door shut and the car tears off, the Gabe lad in front kept twisting round to shout at me, *hey, buck, calm down, we know your brother, we know Cillian, we're mates with Cillian.* I didn't understand because I wasn't doing anything, he was roaring at me like I'd started up on them and they were trying to calm me down. They kept going on about Cillian, how they knew him and his crew and they were all old buddies and all that, and I just sat there, you know, I wasn't fighting or anything, because I knew that bit was true, but I didn't understand what was going on. I thought they were taking me *to* Cillian, but I clocked we were flying off out of town and then I did start freaking out a bit, I started asking them what was going on, telling them how I wanted to get home, and then the Sketch lad started hitting me again and told me to put my head down between my legs and stay like that or he'd kill me, he said.' Doll nodded. 'Kill me. That's what he said. Then we just drove in the dark until we got here.'

Dev thought that this might be the moment in which Doll would make another appeal, another plea to be let go, or for access to a phone. But he said nothing, just bent his head and continued tending to Georgie. Georgie's eyes were closed, his body tucked limp into Doll's groin; there ensconced, the dog appeared to have fallen asleep.

'I never even had a pet,' Doll said, 'but animals like me.'

Dev listened and he heard the sedate thrumming of the animal's breathing resonating out of his tiny chest, a sound that signalled total content. Maybe it wasn't that Doll reminded Georgie of the mother at all. It was just that Doll was here, another body, who had stepped into the space made by the mother's absence, whose presence had permitted Georgie to reactivate all the old circuits of excitement and play and ingratiation rendered dormant by her passing. It occurred to Dev, if not for the first time, it was the first time he had given it meaningful consideration, that Georgie, too, had been grieving, as long as Dev had, if a dog could be said to grieve, and surely it could.

He looked out the window, at the utterly still and blank sky, the counter with the three-quarters-gone sleeve of slice pan crinkled up on it, the hob with the dented old metal teapot perched on its ring.

'That tea any use?' he asked Doll.

Doll looked at his cup.

'It's grand, yeah.'

'My mother used to say I never made it right,' Dev said. 'I'd boil the kettle, steep the pot, leave it stewing there on the hob. But I'd always leave it too long or not long enough. She said the problem is I would stand over it, watching it, worrying about it, which I did do, but only because I didn't want to fuck it up. When she'd do the tea, the second she'd the pot landed on the ring she'd be gone, off all around the house doing God knows what and then come back in her own sweet time. But her tea was always perfect. She said it wasn't about paying attention. She said the knack was to not pay attention just the right amount.'

Doll looked at him. Dev smiled.

'The thing is, I never met anyone in my life who paid more attention than that woman,' he said. 'For her, nothing in this world was beneath consideration.'

Noises carried down the hall. Dev could hear the muffle of steps on the stairs. The Ferdias. Doll's head became cocked, tense.

'How's it going to go down?' he said.

'I don't know,' Dev said. He sat up and cleared his throat. Tears quivered in the lashes of his eyes.

Doll had returned his attention to Georgie, moving his hand, tender and brisk, again and again through the dog's fur.

'I don't want to get hurt,' he said.

'No,' Dev said.

That was the last conversation Dev and Doll had on their own. The Ferdias came down for breakfast and the day went by, hour after hour of eventless, nervous waiting, Gabe and Sketch in and out on the phone, Dev doing what he could to make Doll comfortable. That night they did not send Doll to the basement. A little after one in the morning, Gabe told Dev it was time. Dev came out into the drive with them, into the sudden openness of the cool black night air. As the Ferdias bundled Doll into the car Dev ducked down to tell the kid *good luck*. What else could he say?

11

'How's THE baldy cunt?' Cillian said.

'He'll live,' Nicky said.

Cillian smiled and took a drag of his joint. He was sitting in his usual spot on the couch in the sitting room. In front of him on the coffee table, next to the Zen rock garden, was the bulging bulk of Kieron Flynn's olive-green canvas satchel.

'Good,' Cillian said, 'I barely touched the prick.'

'You gave him enough of a lick to warrant sending him to Castlebar General.'

'They sent him to the hospital?'

'They did.'

'A few stitches and that lad'll be grand,' Cillian tutted dismissively, tapping ash into the seashell ashtray balanced on his knee.

'Where did you get the car out of?' Nicky said.

'Never mind about the car. I can get you a car in my sleep,' Cillian said. 'The Guards show?'

'They did.'

'Anything to tell them?'

'Me?'

'Yeah.'

'I told them what I saw, which was nothing.'

'When I saw you stood there with that baldy cunt, smoking, I thought, fuck now, she's elected to pull something dubious here.'

'Dubious?'

'Sticking a spanner in my mother's plan.'

'So it was Sheila's plan?'

'It was.'

'I thought when she rang me you must have put her up to it.'

'The places a mother's mind will go when her babby's in peril.' Cillian grinned. 'So, what did you tell them?'

'Who?'

'The Guards.'

'That I was out there having a smoke with Flynn, but that I went back inside just before he got attacked, so I didn't hear or see anything.'

'The baldy cunt have anything to tell them?'

'I don't know. The Guards talked to him one on one for a bit, before he got took off in the ambulance.'

'The look on his face when I leapt out of the car,' Cillian said, popping his eyes and dropping his jaw in imitation. 'Gob open, catching flies. Man hadn't a clue.'

After Nicky closed the service door, she had gone straight down the hall and back out onto the restaurant floor. She had taken the jug of water by the greeting stand and went table to table, topping up glasses and asking the guests if she could get them anything else, doing her best to keep her grip on the jug handle steady and her voice level, even as a dire knot was twisting in her guts. She had wanted to go back out to the car park but knew she could not, even though there was no saying how hurt Flynn could be; you could not put anything past Cillian. Finally, after what had seemed like an eternity, though it was probably no more than five or six minutes, Flynn had come stumbling back inside, a gash on his head, and Nicky, being the first person to notice him, had been able to call out in shock and secret relief.

'How much is in there?' Nicky asked, eyeing the satchel.

'A decent amount.'

'Is it enough?'

'It's going to have to be enough,' Cillian said, sucking air in through his teeth and pushing his hand through his hair.

'So why do I need to be here?'

Once the Guards had arrived, they had cordoned off the car park, shut down the bar, and kept all the staff back to interview each in turn. It was almost three when Nicky got out. She was at home, listlessly picking at a plate of cold noodles, wondering what in the hell she should do next, when Cillian rang her and told her to get over to his as soon as she could.

Cillian sat up in his seat and cleared his throat.

'They want you there.'

'What?'

'Right before I called you, they called me, and asked

was I set. I said I was. They said they would call back later tonight with instructions where to meet. The second they call, I have to be ready to go. And they said you have to be with me.'

'I'm not going anywhere with you,' Nicky said.

'They said you have to. They said it's a condition for the meet.'

Squeezing in on her now was that sudden cornered feeling, like when the man appeared in the back room of the Pearl.

'Why?' she managed.

Cillian sat forward, picked up the rake and began gently drawing furrows in the bowl of sand.

'The logic, I reckon, is that you're a civilian,' he said. 'You're outside this situation the way none of the rest of us are. The men who took Doll, they're understandably worried about how things might go down. Now I'm not going to pull something reckless, but they can't be sure about that. So what they're wagering is there's a better chance everything goes off without a hitch if there's a civilian present.'

'Something reckless . . .' Nicky said.

'Nothing's going to happen,' Cillian said. 'We're going to give them their money and they are going to give us Doll. That they even want you there is a good sign. It means they want it to go off without a hitch.'

Nicky was shaking her head.

'I don't want any part of this,' she said.

Cillian slumped back in his seat, his brow pinched.

'I can't make you do anything you don't want to do, young one,' he said with a defusing swick of his hand. 'But that's the condition they set me. I show up without you and it makes them nervous. They get nervous it's more liable things go wrong.'

'I'm hardly going to be any use if things go wrong,' Nicky said.

'If you're there that lowers the chances things will.'

He put down the rake and slapped the satchel, like it was a side of meat.

'Look at what you've done up to now,' he said, his blue eyes looking up at her, boring into her. 'All this is on me. I know that. But I wouldn't ask you if I didn't think you could do it.'

Sara Duane arrived around six. She came into the sitting room carrying a pizza and a bag of chips. She clocked Nicky and managed a thin hello. She looked at Cillian, looked at the satchel on the coffee table, then headed for the kitchen. Cillian followed her. Nicky stayed put, heard the muffled exchanges of their arguing drift down the hallway, heard her own name repeatedly invoked by Sara and Cillian's low, stern responses.

'I can't believe any of this,' Sara said to Nicky when she and Cillian returned to the sitting room. 'You're not actually going through with this?'

Nicky did not know what to say.

'You cannot have this child involved,' Sara declared to Cillian.

'She's already involved,' Cillian said.

Nicky turned down the offer of something to eat but Sara made her take a bit of pizza and chips. They ate in the sitting room. Cillian turned the TV on, just to have some noise and distraction.

Eight o'clock came, nine. Without Nicky having explicitly agreed, it seemed to be accepted that she was participating in whatever was going down tonight.

Near ten, her brother Connor texted.

Craic? he wrote.

None at all, she replied. *Where are you now?*

Twenty minutes later he replied *Little town outside rotterdam*

Any use?

Largely shite no good bars

When u home?

Back wed

C u then

All good?

Yes, she typed without hesitation.

Later

Later

The TV babbled on and no one paid much attention. The atmosphere was funereal. Cillian intermittently revived a piteous stream of small talk that Nicky had no interest in pursuing and which seemed only to antagonise Sara further. Cillian nursed a beer and smoked several joints. Nicky took a few hits because otherwise she would have gone insane.

A mobile started ringing. Nicky lifted her head up. She realised she had dozed off in her chair, one eye crushed into the heel of her palm. Yellow stars boiled and sputtered in her field of vision as Cillian strode off into the hallway with his mobile clamped to his ear. Then he came back in.

'Time to go,' he told Nicky.

Cillian had ditched the car he had used for the robbery earlier, so they took Nicky's.

'Where are we going?' Nicky said as they left Glen Gardens.

'Belleek Wood. There's an access road behind the manor leads out to a spot. I've met them there before,' Cillian said. He was sitting next to her, the satchel stuffed down into the footwell in front of him.

The town was completely deserted, the street lights bathing the night air in a yellow glow so hazy it seemed a kind of malign diffusing gas. The only other signs of life were the traffic lights changing colours with eerie punctuality above the empty junctions.

'You think these men—' Nicky said.

'The Ferdias,' Cillian said.

'—the Ferdias, you think they'll hurt Doll?'

'I don't know, Hennigan, I don't what they'll do,' Cillian said, craning agitatedly forward in his seat and bringing his face right up to the windscreen, like there was something out on the road he needed to see. He hung there like that for a good half-minute. Then, in a mild voice, he said, 'Do you love my brother?'

Nicky flexed her fingers around the rim of the steering wheel. Scared and strung tight as she was, she almost laughed at the apparent earnestness of the query.

'What do you mean?' she said.

'I mean do you love him?'

'I'm going out with him,' she said, 'I hardly hate him, do I?'

'You can love someone and hate them.'

'That's awful philosophical.'

'That's fridge magnet poetry is what that is. Though it happens to be true. You didn't answer my question.'

'Do you love Sara?'

'Absolutely I do.'

'Then I guess I do, too.'

'Doll's a good kid.'

'He is.'

'He thinks the world would run smooth if people just got along.'

'That's not the worst thing to think.'

'In theory, no. But then there's how it actually goes. The thing about Doll is it's already in his nature to get along with people. Or to try to. But there's people in this world should never be in the same room together.'

Nicky was looking straight ahead but she could feel Cillian's attention on her.

'You agree with me, I think,' he said.

They were coming up to a turn for the main road into the manor grounds.

'This way?' Nicky said.

'Straight in,' Cillian said. 'Anyway, what I mean to say is, you're awful good for tolerating me on his behalf.'

'It's not a case of tolerating you,' she bluffed.

'Believe it or not, I know what I'm like,' Cillian said. Now Nicky did look at him. He was still leaning forward

out of his seat, watching the road, smiling brittlely. 'Every
so often, it dawns on me, in cold horror.'

Nicky entered the grounds of Belleek Manor and followed
the drive up the long incline of the vast front lawn, the
grass meticulous and metallic in the blue moonlight. At
the summit of the lawn was the manor itself. It had been
built centuries ago, by a lord lieutenant. A pair of electric
lanterns were burning above the doors of the main
entrance. Save for a single light in the upper-left row of
the building, the windows of all the rooms were lightless
black cavities. The manor was as immense and still as a
foundered liner.

She continued around to the car park.

'Over there, see that gap for the road,' Cillian said.

She took the road he indicated. It was dark and narrow
and unlit, winding through intervals of crowded, over-
hanging branches, and it extended on in this lonely fashion
just long enough to make Nicky begin to doubt that they
were going the right way, or any way at all, before the tiny
black-and-yellow diamond of a road sign flashed in the
headlights and began to grow larger.

'That it?' Nicky said.

'That's it,' Cillian said.

When they got closer, she could see that the sign was
posted by the entrance to a small lay-by.

'Are they there?' Nicky asked as she turned the car in.
The lay-by was completely unlit, a black negative space.

'They're here,' Cillian said in a small, tight voice. Nicky
saw the unlit, dull ruby tail light of a parked car in the

sweep of her headlights. There was a man by the car, just standing there in the dark.

'Oh God,' she heard herself say out loud.

'You're OK,' Cillian said, not looking at her, his attention fixed entirely on the figure by the car, but she could hear a rasping, hysterical edge in his voice too.

She brought the car to a halt but did not cut the engine. The man walked over, stopped several feet short of Cillian's side of the car and stared inside. His face was not hidden. The sleeves of his top appeared to end in nothing, and it took a moment for Nicky's mind, slowing with fear the way cold slows your limbs, to process that his hands were tucked into the pockets of his trousers. The thought struck her that anything might happen now.

'Kill the engine,' the man said, his raised voice dampened by the glass.

Cillian looked at her.

'Turn off the car,' he said.

Nicky killed the ignition and the man stepped closer.

'Put down the window.'

Cillian rolled the window down. The man came in closer again, cocked his head. He was stocky, with slicked-back hair and calm blue eyes flickering in quick minute movements in the sockets of his still face.

'Fucking hell,' he said. 'You brought the young one with you. Unbelievable.'

Cillian glanced guiltily at Nicky and then back at the man. Cillian's spiel insisting they wanted her here. It wasn't them, Nicky realised; it was Cillian wanted a civilian present.

'Where's Doll?' Cillian said quickly.

'Where's the money?' the man replied.

'Right here,' Cillian said, gesturing carefully at the footwell.

'Go on,' the man said.

Cillian reached down and brought up the satchel.

'Where's Doll?' Cillian repeated.

'I'll take you to him.'

The man took a step back.

Cillian got out.

'You too, young one,' the man said.

Nicky's fingers were resting on the key. For a moment she considered turning the car back on, gunning the engine and peeling out of there. Doll be damned. Let all this be Cillian's problem. She looked at Cillian and the man. The man was watching her intently and without apprehension, like he knew exactly what was in her mind.

'Come on,' he said.

Nicky stepped out into the night and pocketed her keys.

'Over here,' the man said.

'This fella here is Sketch Ferdia,' Cillian said as she came around to the other side of the car. 'Sketch and Gabe Ferdia. They're who took Doll.'

'You think you're as clever,' the man, Sketch, said to Cillian. He indicated the satchel. 'Let's have a look, so.'

Cillian undid the buckles, let the top of the bag spout open. Sketch studied the contents. It was filled with plastic bags full of notes and a large Ziploc bag bulging with smaller bags of coins. Sketch removed a hand from a pocket and lifted out the big bag of coins.

'What the fuck is this?' he said, but instead of waiting for an answer dropped the bag back into the satchel. He came around behind Cillian and Nicky, turned on his phone's light and aimed it at a narrow dirt path cutting through the brush. 'Let's go,' he said.

The path led away from the lay-by and into the woods, its trail rising and curving through the thin black masses of the trees. She could smell Cillian as they walked together, the powdery, sour odour of stale sweat. Twice he stumbled in the dark and pulled up cursing. Sketch silently tolerated these interruptions, each time only stopping and waiting for Cillian to get going again.

Nicky knew she should have been enraged at Cillian for luring her here, for trapping her here with him, but as he stumbled along beside her she felt nothing, not even contempt. The moment she stepped out of her car she had crossed a line, that razor-thin border separating the possible from the actual. That crossing was irrevocable, and now that it was done, all of the reasons that had obliged her to do so, including Cillian's duplicitousness, no longer mattered. All that mattered was what would happen next. As she made her way over the uneven ground, her mind was racing, lit up with fragments of animal premonition. She knew violence was close, could sense with each step the approach of some dark, whipping torsion of bodies and limbs that might sweep her up and buffet her away with the powerful headlong indifference of the sea.

And yet even as one part of her mind was tormented by these intimations, another part of her remained strangely calm and blank, had receded into some inner space of resigned and drowsy quiescence. She was scared and she was exhausted. She felt like if she were permitted to lie down on the ground for even a moment, she would fall asleep within seconds.

They kept going and going and finally they emerged into some kind of clearing. The ground became level and grassy underfoot, the clearing bound on its far side by a large formation of rock protruding out of a hill. There were two figures standing by the rock. In the drilling brightness of Sketch's phone light Nicky saw a face, pale and apparitional.

'Doll,' she said.

'That's my brother,' she heard Cillian call out.

Next to Doll was the skinny man from the Pearl, Gabe Ferdia. Gabe was holding a fistful of the hoodie Doll was wearing.

'What the fuck is this?' Gabe said, nodding at Nicky.

'Bringing the beoir. He thinks he's awful clever,' Sketch said.

He snatched the satchel from Cillian and emptied it onto the ground. The bag of coins landed with a jingling thunk amid the smaller bags stuffed with notes.

'How'd you manage this?' Gabe said.

'I robbed a bar,' Cillian said.

'Is it all there?'

Cillian hesitated, said nothing.

'Count it,' Gabe said to Sketch.

Sketch went down onto his haunches. He could not hold the phone and count the money at the same time.

'I need help with the light,' he said.

'Help out that man, young one,' Gabe said to Nicky.

It was OK, Nicky thought. This Gabe man was an evil man, but she grasped that out of everyone here, he was the one who most understood the situation, and she understood that the best chance for everyone else was for things to go how he wanted. Now he had given her an order, and that order had become part of the situation, a part she was responsible for, so she obeyed.

She took Sketch's phone and held it above his shoulder. She pushed aside the racing churn of her thoughts, the sick tight feeling in her nerves, and concentrated on keeping the light steady. All she had to do was keep the light steady.

Sketch was going hastily through the bags, shaking the notes out. Some of the notes were rubber-banded in piles, some were loose. Flynn always tallied the takings by separating the notes out into their denominations and bagging them up. Sketch was dumping them all out together, mixing them up, sliding random handfuls of notes through his fingers with such rapidity Nicky doubted he was counting them in any accurate way before he set them aside.

'What you reckon?' Gabe asked eventually.

'I'm not counting them coins,' Sketch complained.

'Besides them.'

'Yeah,' he muttered, once his own silence had gone on too long, 'I don't fucking know. I reckon there's north of ten grand anyways.'

'It's three short,' Cillian said. 'There's fourteen grand in notes, and them coins come to the guts of six hundred quid. I counted every one of the fuckers this afternoon. It's three and a bit short of the eighteen.'

'Blood from a fucking stone,' Gabe said.

'Sara gets paid this Friday. I can get you the rest then.'

'Oh, you can, can you? At your own fucking conveni-
ence?'

'I'm good for it.'

That did it. Gabe jerked his fist forward and let go of
Doll.

'Go on now, young fella,' he said.

Doll stumbled across to Nicky. She took hold of his
arm. The clothes they had on him were loose and baggy.
He smelled like someone else.

'What are you doing here?' he said wonderingly.

'Cillian wanted me to come,' was all she could think
to say.

Nicky felt a whoosh of movement and looked just in
time to catch Gabe darting forward to swing a fist up into
Cillian's stomach. In the beam of Sketch's phone light, she
watched Cillian double over and drop to his knees with a
gasp. Sketch instantly shot up off the ground, came swiftly
around the side of Cillian and punched him in the temple,
then several times more on the neck until Cillian was down
on his side, curled on the ground with his knees drawn up
to his stomach and his arms wrapped over his head.

'After all this you still have the temerity to show up three
grand short,' Gabe snarled and began kicking at Cillian's
midriff, hurling his foot repeatedly into Cillian's knees.
Sketch was more deliberate. He stepped back, trotted
around to a different angle and studied Cillian's squirming
form before raining a round of measured stamps onto his
thigh and ribs and head.

'They're going to kill him,' Doll cried.

'Stay here,' she said, lacing her arm around his and holding him in place, even though he had not actually made a move.

The two of them stood there and watched as the Ferdias continued to kick and punch at Cillian. It seemed to go on for some time, Cillian curled tightly into a ball as their assaults proceeded in flurries of shortening duration. Eventually, Gabe's breaths grew heavier, and his blows became intermittent and listless. Sketch, as if mindful that his brother was waning, became more perfunctory in his assaults too. The beating came to a stop and the two brothers just stood there, looking at what they had done. Cillian was lying still on the ground.

'*I'm good for it* – that should be your motto, you fucking prick,' Gabe spat. He bent down low and steered his face in close to Cillian's.

'Are you alive?' he said, tapping at his cheek.

Cillian moaned and briefly raised his head.

'Was that shit about the turlough real?'

Cillian was in a bad way. He grunted and tried to lift himself up onto his elbow. Nicky could see his face in profile. It was dark, dirty with blood.

'Maybe it was,' Gabe said, 'maybe it was all down to pure bad luck, but it's about how you play it. I don't know what you thought was going to happen. I don't know where you thought the road you elected to take was going to bring you. But I'm sick of you now, do you hear me? I'm sick of having to think about you. I'm sick of having to look at your face. I'm even sick of bating the head off you.

I don't want to do any of it any more. I want you gone –
are you listening?'

Gabe slapped Cillian's face.

'Yeah, yeah,' Cillian managed.

'I don't ever want to see you around Ballina no more.
Get out of here. Go away. Go join your oul fella in fucking
Canada or wherever the fuck he is. Go where you like.
Only I don't want you here no more.'

As Gabe was saying all this to Cillian, Sketch had squat-
ted back down and was stuffing the money back into the
satchel. Then he stood up and came over to Nicky.

'Phone,' he said.

She handed it over. Sketch turned off the light. The
darkness that fell around them was instantaneous.

'If you've any brains, young one,' Nicky heard Gabe say,
'you'll run a mile in the other direction from this crowd. If
you don't, they'll drag you right down with them.'

Nicky stayed where she was, her arm around Doll's. She
sensed movement, glimpsed in the corner of her eye sudden divisions in the dark that sealed back up as soon as she
looked squarely at them. She held her breath and believed
she could hear the brushy crackle of steps moving away
from them. Doll's arm still in her grasp. Then the only
noise she could hear was the laboured rasps of Cillian, low
on the ground. Slowly, carefully, she slid her free hand
into her pocket and touched the edge of her phone. It had
a light too. She would take it out and turn it on, just as
soon as she was sure the Ferdias were gone for good.

12

DEV WAS on the couch when he heard the car pull up the drive. Georgie leapt from the red wingback chair, completed an urgent circle and scutted away off into the hall barking officiously, already back to his old truculent self.

'You're OK, you're OK,' Dev said, nudging him out of the way of the door.

'Well, young Devereaux,' Gabe declared as he stepped into the hall.

The Ferdias barrelled through into the kitchen. Sketch was carrying what looked like a school bag. He dumped the school bag on the kitchen table. Gabe popped open the fridge, scanned the shelves, and sighed.

'There's not a drop left in this house, is there?' he said, eyeing the cupboards disconsolately.

'You're the ones drank it all,' Dev said. 'How'd it go?'

'It went off beautifully, fella,' Gabe said.

'Doll is gone?'

'Doll English has been returned to the custody of his

brother, God help him.' Gabe took a glass down out of the cupboard. He ran the tap cold, filled the glass, and drank the water down in one long draught. Then he placed the middle finger of his right hand under the tap and winced.

'Think I broke my finger on that cunt's head,' he said.

'I reckon you might have,' Sketch said, 'your form's atrocious.'

'Who got hit?' Dev said.

'I might have left a few on the English buck,' Gabe admitted.

'That fucking cunt!' Sketch exclaimed. 'You know what he did, Dev? He roped in the kid's beoir, had her right there with him.'

'Doll's beoir?'

'Yeah!'

'Why?'

'Insurance, I reckon,' Gabe said. 'Have someone else there in case we'd planned to light the two of them up.'

'Credit to him, the gutless shite,' Sketch jeered.

'But it all went off OK? He brought the money?' Dev said.

'He was three short!' Sketch exclaimed with renewed exasperation. He tore open the buckles of the school bag and started pulling out plastic bags filled with money.

'Straight up admitted it. *I'm good for it*, he said, which set this fella off something rotten,' Sketch said, nodding at Gabe.

'I told him I don't ever want to see him around Ballina again,' Gabe said.

'You think he'll heed you?' Dev said.

'We took the kid and we gave back the kid,' Gabe said. 'That's a gift, that's a mercy, and at the same time, it's showing him exactly how far we can take it if we have to. So, he better fucking heed me.'

'Feel that,' Sketch said, tossing a fat bag of coins at Dev.

Dev caught it. It was heavy.

'That's the weight of six hundred euros in shrapnel, allegedly,' he said.

'Where'd he get this out of?' Dev said.

'Robbed a pub, he said.'

'What pub?'

Sketch shrugged.

'Make sure and get the paper this week,' he said. 'I'm sure it'll get a lively write-up in the *Western*.'

Gabe was back checking the cupboards again.

'There really is no more drink in this house?' he said.

'I told you,' Dev said.

'You've the soul of an abstinent, Dev.'

'I take a drink.'

'You do, but your heart's not in it.'

'So, what are you going to do now?' Dev said.

Gabe turned and folded his arms and propped himself against the countertop.

'Cleanest thing might be for us to get out of dodge ourselves for a little while, just until we're sure the dust has settled,' he said.

'Imagine that prick gets sent down for robbing a pub,' Sketch said.

'I was thinking Marbella, is what I was thinking,' Gabe said.

'Marbella'd be nice,' Sketch concurred.

'Floating in the pool on a lilo, sipping on a big oul sangria, letting the sun cook me like a rotisserie chicken.'

'Spanish fanny,' Sketch drawled wistfully.

The brothers cackled. They were giddy and relieved and satisfied with themselves.

'Would you fancy coming along with us, Dev?' Sketch said. 'Sangria and sand, and more silly bitches in bikinis than you'd ever know what to do with.'

'I don't think,' Dev said, 'that'd be my thing.'

'Fair enough,' Sketch conceded with a grin.

'There was something else, though,' Gabe said.

'What?' Dev said.

'This arrangement we have going. Mulrooney was reckoning' – Gabe's voice dipped and he cleared his throat – 'he was thinking it might be best to put the operation on ice for the moment. He didn't want us to tell you until this shite with the English buck was sorted.'

'Mulrooney wants to put the arrangement on ice?'

'For a while,' Gabe said. 'The thing is, the margins were always thin out here anyway, and they're only getting thinner. Back in the boom times, when every two-bit car dealer in Swinford was looking to get tuned up at the weekend, you could just about justify an operation this rural, but the truth is the local market's been fucked since the crash. It's been touch and go for a while, even before this episode with English.'

'So all this is done with?' Dev said.

'You can keep that,' Sketch said, nodding at the bag of

coins Dev was still holding. 'Go in and put a few bets on the dogs for you and your oul fella.'

'I don't want a bag of coins.'

'Do what you like with it,' Gabe said coldly, 'bury it in the backyard, give it straight back to Cillian English. It's yours.'

Sketch packed the rest of the money up and stood up from the table.

'You didn't think we were gonna do it, Dev, did ya?'

'There's nothing I'd put past you,' Dev said.

'That was some few days,' Sketch continued. 'What the fuck were we thinking? But we pulled it off.'

The brothers headed down the hall, towards the front door.

Dev left the bag of coins down on the table and followed them. He could not believe that it was over.

'This is what Mulrooney wants?' he said.

Gabe placed his hand on the latch of the door and paused. He considered the coat rack heaped with coats, the hallway wallpaper.

'You know, you got the bones of a decent place here, lad. You have money. You should do it up a bit. Property at your age. There's not many can say that. It's not the worst, lad.'

'We had a good run,' Sketch said. 'And you never let us down, Dev. You're a stone-cold cunt.'

Georgie bristled by Dev's foot, addressed several barks at the Ferdias' legs. Gabe stooped and grinned in Georgie's face.

'You I'll miss like a hole in the head,' he said, chucking

Georgie under the chin. Then he stood up and opened the door. The Ferdia brothers stepped outside and the light came on in the drive. The black night air was fresh, summer-mild.

'I'll be here,' Dev said.

'We know you will,' Gabe said.

Dev hung by the door and watched their backs as they crunched across to the car, the pale gold flicker of the script on Gabe's jacket. TEQUILA PATROL. He stood there until the Ferdias' car had disappeared down the drive.

He went back into the kitchen. He rinsed and put away the glass Gabe had used. He opened the crinkled bag of bread on the counter. One slice and a crust were all that was left. He would have to do a shop tomorrow; there was always a shop. He was hungry but he tossed the two slices of bread into Georgie's basket. The dog gratefully clambered in and began eating.

He took a seat at the table, the bag of coins planted there in the middle of it. He looked around the empty kitchen. A part of him wanted this of course. A part of him had always wanted this, to be alone, away from even the prospect of any demand upon him to talk, to interact, to acknowledge opinions and be expected to offer ones in return, to be responsible for anyone but himself and the dog. To be left be. To be.

His head still hurt, that rooted, ineradicable throb in the meaty centre of his skull. He blinked and saw motes. His pulse flickered. He stood up to get the medicine box and was hit by a smell. For a moment he was sure it was the ghostly stink of Gabe's feet, then he realised the smell was coming from him, ripe and clinging. He counted back the days. He had not showered since before they showed up with Doll.

He checked but the paracetamol was all gone.

'I'm going to take a shower,' he said.

Georgie looked up, whimpered, and returned to his meal.

Upstairs, Dev let the water run hot. Though he and the kid had swept up all the glass and debris from the floor and put back up the shower rod, the bathroom was still in bad shape. The cabinet above the sink was an emptied-out cavity, its metal frame mirrorless and buckled, framing nothing.

Dev went into his room. He sat down on the end of his bed. The tightness was there in his chest, a smattering of silver motes drifting at the edges of his vision. He was remembering how, after the night he went to the quarry, his mother took him to the GP. Not their usual family GP, doddering old Dr Gardner with his enormous ties and genteelly derisive manner, but another GP. Dr Helen Scarlet was a woman in her thirties. When he and the mother went in to meet her, Dev remembers that Dr Scarlet had her hair up, a pair of thin, needle-like sticks crossed in an X through the caramel knot of her bun. She saw Dev come lumbering in through the door and she did not react; no mortified second take or incredulous steepling of her brow. She just took him in and bid him sit down and introduced herself. After a couple of preliminaries, in which Dev's mother, strenuously deploying as many euphemisms as she could, outlined Dev's *recent troubles*, Dr Scarlet began to ask him a series of questions, some direct and specific, some broad and general. As she did this, Dev watched her reach up and withdraw one stick from her bun and reinsert it at a slightly different angle. He remembered that Dr Scarlet elaborated this gesture gently, not taking her eyes off Dev the entire time. It struck him, thinking about it later, that this gesture had denoted not a diversion of her attention, but an intensification of it. To her questions, Dev stuttered bereftly through what seemed to him, even as he related them, a succession of fragmentary, incoherent and inadequate non-answers. Nonetheless, Dr Scarlet listened carefully and assured Dev that he had done the right thing by coming in to see her. She said she was recommending a prescription of antidepressant and anxiety medications, to be started right away; additionally, she suggested an initial course of outpatient counselling, once a week, for eight weeks.

Half the reason Dev agreed to the counselling was that he had assumed, stupidly and prematurely, that the sessions would be with Dr Scarlet. Instead, every Wednesday afternoon, he ascended to the anonymous second-floor hallway of the GPs', where he squeezed himself into a small, barely furnished, deskless room across from one of the most slender and delicately proportioned men Dev had ever seen in his life. The man had apple-cheeked, elfin features and a shock of ginger hair. Dev was only seventeen but the man, purportedly in his twenties, looked younger that him. Dr Jarleth had an unplaceable mild Midlands accent. He wore the top three buttons of his shirt open and had a long, startlingly pale neck. When he was nervous, or just at a loss, he would touch his neck and emit a single dry giggle. It was a kind of punctuation. He was either a psychologist or a psychiatrist, or maybe just a general therapist, if there was such a thing; in any case, he may well not have been a doctor at all but Dev always addressed him as Doctor. Jarleth never corrected him.

Each session lasted an hour. Dev's sense was that Dr Jarleth was not very experienced. His manner veered between tentative and callously brisk, between stifling silences and feigned cheer. Often, he could not hide how bored he was.

At the start of every session Dev was handed a questionnaire, which he filled out while Dr Jarleth stepped from the room for five minutes. The one window was always shut, the room muggy. Dev would quickly begin to get drowsy as he went through the questionnaire, selecting on a scale of one to five the number that best corresponded to the robustness of his libido, the intensity and frequency of his spells of suicidal ideation, the intensity and frequency of his compulsive and/or negative thoughts, the duration and frequency of his insomniacal spells, for that week. Dev tended to race through the questionnaire in a drifting stupor, often not even properly reading the questions. It was all too confusing and vague and abstract. He did not know how to assign numbers to the things happening inside himself, and in addition he began to nurse a steepening suspicion that the numbers he did submit were being collected for an ulterior purpose, in order to be eventually used against him – if things did not change, if he did not start getting *better*, whatever *better* might mean in this context. So half the time he circled numbers at random, just to get this exercise over and done with, but as soon as Dr Jarleth returned to the room and took the completed questionnaire off Dev and added it to the laminate pouch in the grey ring binder in which he kept all of the questionnaires he had previously collected from Dev, Dev would immediately begin to fixate and brood upon a particular question he was sure he had taken up the wrong way, subsequently becoming too distracted to pay proper heed to Jarleth as he tried to talk to Dev about how his week had gone and where his head was at and how things were at home.

After the eight weeks were finally done, Dr Jarleth recommended a follow-up course of counselling several months hence and Dev initially agreed, but when the time came, he fobbed it off. By then he had got the job in Complere and was happy with it. Out of the house every day making money, even going for drinks at the weekend with his workmates. He was able to convince his mother there was nothing else he needed from the counselling.

He never saw Dr Jarleth again after that. Maybe the sessions had helped, though Dev was left with the nagging impression that whatever it was he was supposed to have achieved, he had surely failed to. Certain moments stuck with him, like the time Jarleth, who, whatever his other issues, was generally disciplined about not burdening Dev with unsolicited opinions, cut into some long-winded and no doubt completely banal story or anecdote Dev was in the middle of recounting and told him, 'What you are in, Dev, is a holding pattern, only you're not holding out for anything.'

Dev remembers the pink flush that seized Dr Jarleth's face as soon as he made this statement. Realising he had evidently overstepped some mark, he took a nervous sip of his water and cleared his throat, touched his neck and giggled.

'I'm sorry, Dev,' he said. 'That really wasn't a criticism. I hope you didn't hear it as such.'

'It never occurred to me it was,' Dev remembers telling him.

It was Dr Jarleth who taught Dev about the counting and the breaths, whenever he felt an attack coming on. It was Dr Jarleth who taught him about touching a solid and/or textured surface, concentrating on the concreteness and particularity of a given surface, these extensions of the solid world that was all around him and that wanted and required nothing of him, but was just there, felt and secure.

The shower was still going. Dev's bedroom door was open. He could hear the water across the hall. He reminded himself that he had come upstairs to have a shower, so he was going to shower. He bent down and worked off one of his huge socks. He lifted his foot onto his knee and examined it, the thick, yellow-tinged nails with their lengthening white ends. As he shifted his position, he noticed that the feeling in his chest had changed. There was now a clotted, buzzing quality to the sensation. He was having an attack, yes, but not a strong one, and it had already passed its acutest point.

Because he was alone, he almost hadn't noticed.

He was tired.

His body was tired.

He felt it all around him.

Think of your body as a machine. A machine has its processes, Jarleth had said.

Dev thought about how little you had to do with your body, really; it was true that it had its routines and processes, most of which were benign and necessary, but some of which were catastrophic and inexplicable. And the thing was, it perpetuated those processes irrespective of your wishes. He thought about how, when it came down to it, you were a kind of janitor or superintendent of your body, responsible only for its sanitation and presentation. You fuelled it and disposed of its waste, showered it, dressed it. You brushed its hair and you cut its nails. But you could choose not to do these things and your body, regardless of your neglect, would simply carry on for as long as it could.

He listened to the drumming of the shower into the empty basin of the bath, and realised, with a familiar twinge of self-recrimination, that the water had been running so long he could have had two showers by now. For a moment he imagined leaping up and striding into the bathroom, wrenching the spigot and bringing the stream to a startled stop, just forgetting about the whole thing. But he didn't do that either. Instead, he just kept staring at his foot, the cracked folds of hard flesh where his sole curved and turned a chalky white.

He was back where he always seemed to end up. His life, circling, tighter and tighter, in on itself. It was as if every time he tried to move off, however tentatively, in a new direction, he was wrenched right back to the centre of himself. And that centre was getting smaller and smaller, more decrepit and ferociously reduced. His mother gone, the father gone, now even the Ferdias. He thought of Sketch sneering about the bag of coins – *put a few bets on the dogs for you and your oul fella.*

What he couldn't explain was that he didn't even hate his father any more. It was only that he had never been able to find a way to help him, just as his father had never found a way to help Dev. And it was difficult, eventually it was unbearable, to be around someone you could not help, and he had not understood this until it was way, way too late.

The water drumming.

All processes end, Jarleth had said.

He had to stop being like this, he knew.

He had come upstairs because he had wanted to take a shower; now all he needed to do was finish taking off his clothes and get in. He imagined the pressurised jet of water, the firm pleasing rush of it travelling down his head. He wanted to be in the shower already, under the water as the warm enclosing wall of it crashed around him. If he could get clean, and take his pill, and sleep; tomorrow it could all begin to be different. He just needed to get there. But in the meantime, all he could do was keep looking at his foot. It hung there like it had nothing to do with him. And that was the thing. That was what made it all so difficult. You couldn't do anything until you did another thing first.

13

CILLIAN WAS able to get to his feet. Doll slung Cillian's arm over his shoulder and helped him along the path back to the car, Nicky leading the way with the light from her phone. They got Cillian into the back seat. She gunned it back up and out the access road, past the lightless facade and the burning lanterns of Belleek Manor and soon they were out on the main road.

'How you doing back there?' Nicky said. He was lying down, so she couldn't see him in the rear-view. His breathing was shallow, wet and obstructed sounding.

'I'm OK,' he said.

'Maybe we should go to the hospital?' she said.

Doll blinked and looked at her, a doubtful, temporising half-smile on his pale face. Nicky got the sense he had not registered the question.

'Should we take Cillian to the hospital, do you think?' she said again.

'No hospital,' Cillian urged from the back, coughing and groaning.

'You could be in a really bad way,' Doll said suddenly.

'Get to Mam's,' Cillian said.

'We could call an ambulance from there, if he needs it,' Doll said. His tone was flat, calm.

He fanned his hands on the dashboard's leather.

Nicky looked and saw dark, ugly wounds all around his wrists.

'Your wrists,' she said.

'I don't understand why you came,' Doll said to her.

'Cillian,' she began. She heard his thin wheezing in the back as she watched the road, the way it seemed to continuously hurtle and leap up into the glow of the headlights before disappearing beneath the car. The rooftops and driveways of houses began to appear, and a wash of relief came over her as she approached the junction that would bring them back into town.

'Cillian wanted me to,' was all she said.

She glanced again at Doll's wrists.

'What did they do to you, Doll?' she asked. 'Where were you?'

'They slapped me around a bit, all right,' Doll said. 'The worst was they had me tied to the bed at night. It was awful trying to get to sleep.'

Doll spoke these sentences without any great feeling, only an eerie peaceableness.

'But where were you?' she repeated.

'They had me at this house,' he said. 'They put me in the basement.'

'Whose house?'

'He wasn't the worst,' Doll said. 'The other two were making him do it.'

'Whose house were you in?' Cillian managed from the back.

'Fella named Dev. Dev Hendrick,' Doll said. 'A big lad.'

'Dev Hendrick?' Cillian said. 'Dev Hendrick?'

He managed a laugh, and Nicky heard him moving, pulling himself upright in his seat.

'Dev fucking Hendrick was the biggest fucking gaum going in that school,' he said.

'You know this fella?' Nicky said to Cillian.

'That poor bastard,' Cillian said. 'The size of him and he never used to stand up for himself. They used to kick seven shades of shite out of him. I can't believe the Ferdias had that fucking gaum in on this.'

Doll turned around and looked at Cillian.

'Did you really rob a bar?' he said.

As if from very far away it came back to Nicky that the Pearl had been robbed, that Cillian had done it and that Flynn was in the hospital. *Imagine if we took you to the hospital and you ended up in the bed next to Flynn*, she felt like roaring at Cillian. It was a joke how tangled and confused everything was.

'He robbed the Pearl,' Nicky said.

'What?' Doll said.

'It's true.' Cillian coughed and laughed.

Nicky glanced in the mirror. Cillian's lip was all torn. Blood was caked into his brow and had dried in streaks on his face. He looked like he'd a pot of motor oil tipped over his head.

'They did some number on you,' Nicky said.

'I don't even feel too bad, now,' Cillian said with sudden energy. 'I mean I feel like total shit, but I don't feel too bad.'

Soon they were out of the town centre and onto the Killala road. The horizon rode flat and low either side of the car, a clear night full of stars pressing down.

'I can't believe you came to get me,' Doll said to Nicky. 'I'm sorry I was a prick to you on Friday night, you know.'

'Never mind a thing about Friday night,' Nicky said.

'The mother's going to freak,' Cillian said with a note of dark, almost pleasurable anticipation in his voice. 'She won't believe her eyes.'

'Was Mam worrying?' Doll asked.

Cillian let out a dazed, splintery laugh.

'What do you think, kid?' he said.

They were passing the bog. Moonlight glimmered in its dark ruts and channels, like a lake. Doll was looking out at it.

'They wouldn't let me call Mam,' he said. 'All the time I wanted to call her, just so she'd know not to worry. But I couldn't because they took my phone.'

Nicky thought of the calls she'd made to Doll the Friday and Saturday, the messages she'd left, the way her anger had cooled into complacency.

'Well, that wasn't your fault,' she said.

They came to the Killala Bay Hotel. There were low hills behind it, the hill's ridges edged with the silhouettes of conifers. The trees belonged to Belleek Wood, too. The wood stretched from town to here and then continued all the way down to Killala Bay itself.

When they pulled into the drive of the English house, Nicky parked as usual by the hedge. She got out and slid her seat forward to let Cillian out. He gripped her offered forearm and clambered gingerly from the car. He was able to stand by himself. Nicky ducked her head back in. Doll was sitting stock-still in the passenger seat, staring into the hedge, as if deep in consideration.

'You all right?' she asked gently, aware of how daft that question was as she asked it.

He did not answer. She looked at what he was looking at. It was more or less the spot where the old Umbro ball had been embedded, the ball that she had pulled out of there and tossed in the bin on Friday night. She wondered if that was what Doll was staring so perplexedly at, the ball that was no longer there.

'Your mother's just inside,' she said to him, and as she did the door rattled on its hinges and she looked up to see Sheila in her pyjamas racing from the house.

'Oh Lord Jesus,' she exclaimed. 'Oh dear God in heaven.'

She came straight up to Cillian. She reached and touched him on the forehead like she was feeling him for a fever.

'I got Doll back,' he said.

'You need a doctor—' Sheila said.

'I don't need a doctor. I said I got Doll back.'

He took her by the elbow and motioned towards the car. It was only then she seemed to understand what he was saying. Sheila came over to the passenger side, stooped and looked in through the window.

'Oh my sweet Jesus,' she said.

She started working the door handle, but it was locked from the inside.

'Give me a second, Mam,' Nicky heard Doll announce. His tone was strange, almost sharp. Sheila let go of the handle and took a step back and waited. After a moment, Doll popped the door and got out. Sheila hugged him.

'There you are,' she moaned into his shoulder.

'I'm OK,' he said. 'It's all right, Mam.'

'The lad's in shock,' Cillian said, and Nicky realised he was right.

'Are you hurt?' Sheila asked Doll, feeling him down along his arms.

'I'm OK.'

She lifted his hands and saw the dark wounds around his wrists.

'Oh, my darling,' she said.

'It looks worse than it is,' Doll said.

Now Sheila took a step back from Doll and released him.

'Nicky,' Sheila said, taking one of Nicky's hands. 'Are you OK, girl?'

'I am,' Nicky said.

'What you did . . .' Sheila said, her voice cracking and welling up.

'Nerves of steel, this girl,' Cillian said.

Sheila sniffed and threw back her head and a low sigh escaped her lips.

'You OK?' Cillian said.

Sheila touched her temple.

'Just the head.'

'Them migraines still at you?' Cillian said.

'I hit it with every pill I had, but it broke through last night. Stress,' Sheila said, squeezing the back of her neck, 'does not help.'

'What I need now,' Cillian said, 'is a fat joint and a drink of beer. I'd take a drink of the shittiest beer in the world right now.'

'I've nothing like that in the house,' Sheila warned him.

'I didn't figure I was coming inside.'

'Of course you can come inside,' Sheila said, 'if you want.'

Cillian was looking up at the house and grinning wildly.

'It's been a while.'

'It has.'

'They told me go join him. The oul fella.'

'What?'

'The lads who took Doll. They told me to get out of here. Out of Ballina, out of Mayo, out of Ireland. They want me gone for good after this.'

'You got them their money. Is that not it done?'

'It seems me fucking off is part of it getting done,' he said and began limping towards the house.

'Cillian,' Sheila said, catching up with him and tucking her small shoulder under his arm the better to help him along.

'I'm all right,' he said, weakly trying to shake free.

'Will you just stop and let me help you?' Sheila said.

Cillian did.

'Imagine getting all the way to Calgary and showing up at the oul fella's door,' he said, 'telling him I'm on the run from some serious cunts back in Ireland, and I need a place to crash.'

'Oh Lord,' Sheila said, 'I can just imagine the look on his face.'

'We'd have a good night that night, I'd say. But he'd be packed and gone again the next morning.'

They were laughing by now, Sheila and Cillian, in each other's arms, seized by the delirium of relief as she helped him through the front door. She looked back out, to where Nicky was standing with Doll by the car.

'Come in, you two,' she said, 'come in out of the dark.'

'I'll bring him in,' Nicky said.

'Good girl,' Sheila said, then helped Cillian in and down the hall.

Nicky closed the passenger door of the car. She recalled the moment, heading over to Belleek Wood, when Cillian had asked her, seemingly out of the blue, if she loved Doll. Already, she had forgotten what she had said, the particulars of the cagey non-answer she had proffered. The question had triggered a feeling, a recurring, fugitive feeling, one that had been surfacing more and more over the last while, and which Nicky did her best to dispel whenever it did. It had surfaced at Cannon's party, when Marina Scully had suggested Doll might follow her up to Dublin for college, in the quickness with which Nicky asserted she would not want to be the reason. It had surfaced again, later, when she had fought with Doll on the couch, when she had told him *you like things easy.*

'I'm sorry too, you know,' she said.

Doll looked at her, this shook incarnation of him with his pale face and big eyes and strange clothes. The T-shirt he was wearing said NEVERMIND.

'You didn't do anything,' he said.

The feeling would come again and she would push it away again, and on it would go until she could not do it any more. When that day came, everything would change. She knew it would. But for now, that did not matter. What mattered was that Doll was back with his family. And Nicky had helped get him back. All she had to do now was go inside and be with them, for just a little while more.

She looked towards the house. Sheila had left the door open.

'Come on,' Nicky said, taking Doll by the arm, 'they're waiting for us.'

ACKNOWLEDGEMENTS

I would like to thank Katie and Nick for their patience and dedication during the writing of this book. Thank you to Lucy Luck for her unflagging support.

Thank you to my kind and insightful early readers, including Colm Tóibín and Tim MacGabhann.

And all my love to Lucy, Ellie and Daniel.